THE GOVER
OR, THE LITTLE
FEMALE ACADEMY (1749)

by Sarah Fielding

There lived in the northern parts of England, a gentlewoman who undertook the education of young ladies; and this trust she endeavoured faithfully to discharge, by instructing those committed to her care in reading, writing, working, and in all proper forms of behaviour. And though her principal aim was to improve their minds in all useful knowledge; to render them obedient to their superiors, and gentle, kind, and affectionate to each other; yet did she not omit teaching them an exact neatness in their persons and dress, and a perfect gentility in their whole carriage.

This gentlewoman, whose name was Teachum, was the widow of a clergyman, with whom she had lived nine years in all the harmony and concord which forms the only satisfactory happiness in the married state. Two little girls (the youngest of which was born before the second year of their marriage was expired) took up a great part of their thoughts; and it was their mutual design to spare no pains or trouble in their education.

Mr. Teachum was a very sensible man, and took great delight in improving his wife; as she also placed her chief pleasure in receiving his instructions. One of his constant subjects of discourse to her was concerning the education of children: so that, when in his last illness his physicians pronounced him beyond the power of their art to relieve him, he expressed great satisfaction in the thought of leaving his children to the care of so prudent a mother.

Mrs. Teachum, though exceedingly afflicted by such a loss, yet thought it her duty to call forth all her resolutions to conquer her grief, in order to apply herself to the care of these her dear husband's children. But her misfortunes were not here to end: for within a twelvemonth after the death of her husband, she was deprived of both her children by a violent fever that then raged in the country; and, about the same time, by the unforeseen breaking of a banker, in whose hands almost all her fortune was just then placed, she was bereft of the means of her future support.

The Christian fortitude with which (through her husband's instructions) she had armed her mind, had not left it in the power of any outward accident to bereave her of her understanding, or to make her incapable of doing what was proper on all occasions. Therefore, by the advice of all her friends, she undertook what she was so well qualified for; namely, the education of children. But as she was moderate in her desires, and did not seek to raise a great fortune, she was resolved to take no more scholars than she could have an eye to herself without the help of other teachers; and instead of making interest to fill her school, it was looked upon as a great favour when she would take any girl. And as her number was fixed to nine, which she on no account would be prevailed on to increase, great application was made, when any scholar went away, to have her place supplied; and happy were they who could get a promise for the next vacancy.

Mrs. Teachum was about forty years old, tall and genteel in her person, though somewhat inclined to fat. She had a lively and commanding eye, insomuch that she naturally created an awe in all her little scholars; except when she condescended to smile, and talk familiarly to them; and then she had something perfectly kind and tender in her manner. Her temper was so extremely calm and good, that though she never omitted reprehending, and that pretty severely, any girl that was guilty of the smallest fault proceeding from an evil disposition; yet for no cause whatsoever was she provoked to be in a passion; but she kept up such a dignity and authority, by her steady behavior, that the girls greatly feared to incur her displeasure by disobeying her commands; and were equally pleased with her approbation, when they had done anything worthy her commendation.

At the time of the ensuing history, the school (being full) consisted of the nine following young ladies:

Miss JENNY PEACE.   Miss NANNY SPRUCE.   Miss SUKEY JENNETT. Miss BETTY FORD.   Miss DOLLY FRIENDLY.   Miss HENNY FRET.   Miss LUCY SLY.   Miss POLLY SUCKLING.   Miss PATTY LOCKIT.

The eldest of these was but fourteen years old, and none of the rest had yet attained their twelfth year.

AN ACCOUNT OF A FRAY,
BEGUN AND CARRIED ON FOR THE SAKE OF AN APPLE: IN WHICH ARE SHOWN THE SAD EFFECTS OF RAGE AND ANGER.

It was on a fine summer's evening when the school-hours were at an end, and the young ladies were admitted to divert themselves for some time, as they thought proper, in a pleasant garden adjoining to the house, that their governess, who delighted in pleasing them, brought out a little basket of apples, which were intended to be divided equally amongst them; but Mrs. Teachum being hastily called away (one of her poor neighbours having had an accident which wanted her assistance), she left the fruit in the hands of Miss Jenny Peace, the eldest of her scholars, with a strict charge to see that every one had an equal share of her gift.

But here a perverse accident turned good Mrs. Teachum's design of giving them pleasure into their sorrow, and raised in their little hearts nothing but strife and anger: for, alas! there happened to be one apple something larger than the rest, on which the whole company immediately placed their desiring eyes, and all at once cried out, 'Pray, Miss Jenny, give me that apple.' Each gave her reasons why she had the best title to it: the youngest pleaded her youth, and the eldest her age; one insisted on her goodness, another from her meekness claimed a title to preference; and one, in confidence of her strength, said positively, she would have it; but all speaking together, it was difficult to distinguish who said this, or who said that.

Miss Jenny begged them all to be quiet, but in vain; for she could not be heard: they had all set their hearts on that fine apple, looking upon those she had given them as nothing. She told them they had better be contented with what they had, than be thus seeking what it was impossible for her to give to them all. She offered to divide it into eight parts, or to do anything to satisfy them; but she might as well have been silent; for they were all talking and had no time to hear. At last as a means to quiet the disturbance, she threw this apple, the cause of their contention, with her utmost force over a hedge into another garden, where they could not come at it.

At first they were all silent, as if they were struck dumb with astonishment with the loss of this one poor apple, though at the same time they had plenty before them.

But this did not bring to pass Miss Jenny's design: for now they all began again to quarrel which had the most right to it, and which ought to have had it, with as much vehemence as they had before contended for the possession of it; and their anger by degrees became so high, that words could not vent half their rage; and they fell to pulling of caps, tearing of hair, and dragging the clothes off one another's backs: though they did not so much strike, as endeavour to scratch and pinch their enemies.

Miss Dolly Friendly as yet was not engaged in the battle; but on hearing her friend Miss Nanny Spruce scream out, that she was hurt by a sly pinch from one of the girls, she flew on this sly pincher, as she called her, like an enraged lion on its prey; and not content only to return the harm her friend had received, she struck with such force, as felled her enemy to the ground. And now they could not distinguish between friend and enemy; but fought, scratched, and tore, like so many cats, when they extend their claws to fix them in their rival's heart.

Miss Jenny was employed in endeavouring to part them.

In the midst of this confusion appeared Mrs. Teachum, who was returning in hopes to see them happy with the fruit she had given them; but she was some time there before either her voice or presence could awaken them from their attention to the fight; when on a sudden they all faced her, and fear of punishment began now a little to abate their rage. Each of the misses held in her right hand, fast clenched, some marks of victory; for they beat and were beaten by turns. One of them held a little lock of hair torn from the head of her enemy; another grasped a piece of a cap, which, in aiming at her rival's hair, had deceived her hand, and was all the spoils she could gain; a third clenched a piece of an apron; a fourth, of a frock. In short, everyone unfortunately held in her hand a proof of having been engaged in the battle. And the ground was spread with rags and tatters, torn from the backs of the little inveterate combatants.

Mrs. Teachum stood for some time astonished at the sight; but at last she enquired of Miss Jenny Peace, who was the only person disengaged, to tell her the whole truth, and to inform her of the cause of all this confusion.

Miss Jenny was obliged to obey the commands of her governess; though she was so good natured that she did it in the mildest terms; and endeavoured all she could to lessen, rather than increase, Mrs. Teachum's anger. The guilty persons now began all to excuse themselves as fast as tears and sobs would permit them.

One said, 'Indeed, madam, it was none of my fault; for I did not begin; for Miss Sukey Jennett, without any cause in the world (for I did nothing to provoke her), hit me a great slap in the face, and made my tooth ache; the pain DID make me angry; and then, indeed, I hit her a little tap; but it was on her back; and I am sure it was the smallest tap in the world and could not possibly hurt her half so much as her great blow did me.'

'Law, miss!' replied Miss Jennett, 'how can you say so? when you know that you struck me first, and that yours was the great blow, and mine the little tap; for I only went to defend myself from your monstrous blows.'

Such like defences they would all have made for themselves, each insisting on not being in fault, and throwing the blame on her companion; but Mrs. Teachum silenced them by a positive command; and told them, that she saw they were all equally guilty, and as such would treat them.

Mrs. Teachum's method of punishing I never could find out. But this is certain, the most severe punishment she had ever inflicted on any misses, since she had kept a school, was now laid on these wicked girls, who had been thus fighting, and pulling one another to pieces, for a sorry apple.

The first thing she did was to take away all the apples; telling them, that before they had any more instances of such kindness from her, they should give her proofs of their deserving them better. And when she had punished them as much as she thought proper, she made them all embrace one another, and promise to be friends for the future; which, in obedience to her commands, they were forced to comply with, though there remained a grudge and ill-will in their bosoms; every one thinking she was punished most, although she would have it, that she deserved to be punished least; and they continued all the sly tricks they could think on to vex and tease each other.

A DIALOGUE BETWEEN MISS JENNY PEACE AND MISS SUKEY JENNETT;

WHEREIN THE LATTER IS AT LAST CONVINCED OF HER OWN FOLLY IN BEING SO QUARRELSOME; AND, BY HER EXAMPLE, ALL HER COMPANIONS ARE BROUGHT TO SEE AND CONFESS THEIR FAULT.

The next morning Miss Jenny Peace used her utmost endeavours to bring her schoolfellows to be heartily reconciled, but in vain: for each insisted on it, that she was not to blame; but that the whole quarrel arose from the faults of others. At last ensued the following dialogue between Miss Jenny Peace and Miss Sukey Jennett, which brought about Miss Jenny's designs; and which we recommend to the consideration of all our young readers.

MISS JENNY. Now pray, Miss Sukey, tell me, what did you get by your contention and quarrel about that foolish apple?

MISS SUKEY. Indeed, ma'am, I shall not answer you; I know that you only want to prove, that you are wiser than I, because you are older. But I don't know but some people may understand as much at eleven years old as others at thirteen: but, because you are the oldest in the school, you always want to be tutoring and governing. I don't like to have more than one governess; and if I obey my mistress, I think that is enough.

MISS JENNY. Indeed, my dear, I don't want to govern you, nor to prove myself wiser than you; I only want that instead of quarrelling, and making yourself miserable, you should live at peace and be happy. Therefore, pray do answer my question, whether you get anything by your quarrel?

MISS SUKEY. No I cannot say I got anything by it: for my mistress was angry, and punished me; and my hair was pulled off, and my clothes torn in the scuffle; neither did I value the apple; but yet I have too much spirit to be imposed on. I am sure I had as good a right to it as any of the others; and I would not give up my right to anyone.

MISS JENNY. But don't you know, Miss Sukey, it would have shown much more spirit to have yielded the apple to another, than to have fought about it? Then indeed you would have proved your sense; for you would have shown, that you had too much understanding to fight about a trifle. Then your clothes had been whole, your hair not torn from your head, your mistress had not been angry, nor had your fruit been taken away from you.

MISS SUKEY. And so, miss, you would fain prove, that it is wisest to submit to everybody that would impose upon one? But I will not believe ii, say what you will.

MISS JENNY. But is not what I say true? If you had not been in the battle, would not your clothes have been whole, your hair not torn, your mistress pleased with you, and the apples your own?

Here Miss Sukey paused for some time: for as Miss Jenny was in the right and had truth on her side, it was difficult for Miss Sukey to know what to answer. For it is impossible, without being very silly, to contradict truth; and yet Miss Sukey was so foolish, that she did not care to own herself in the wrong; though nothing could have been so great a sign of her understanding.

When Miss Jenny saw her thus at a loss for an answer, she was in hopes of making her companion happy; for, as she had as much good nature as understanding, that was her design. She therefore pursued her discourse in the following manner:

MISS JENNY. Pray, Miss Sukey, do answer me one question more. Don't you lie awake at nights, and fret and vex yourself, because you are angry with your school-fellows? Are not you restless and uneasy, because you cannot find a safe method to be revenged on them, without being punished yourself? Do tell me truly, is not this your case?

MISS SUKEY. Yes it is. For if I could but hurt my enemies, without being hurt myself, it would be the greatest pleasure I could have in the world.

MISS JENNY. Oh fie, Miss Sukey! What you have now said is wicked. Don't you consider what you say every day in your prayers'? And this way of thinking will make you lead a very uneasy life. If you would hearken to me, I could put you into a method of being very happy, and making all those misses you call your enemies, become your friends.

MISS SUKEY. You could tell me a method, miss? Do you think I don't know as well as you what is fit to be done? I believe I am as capable of finding the way to be happy, as you are of teaching me.

Here Miss Sukey burst into tears, that anybody should presume to tell her the way to be happy.

MISS JENNY. Upon my word, my dear, I don't mean to vex you; but only, instead of tormenting yourself all night in laying plots to revenge yourself, I would have you employ this one night in thinking of what I have said. Nothing will show your sense so much, as to own that you have been in the wrong. Nor will anything prove a right spirit so much as to confess your fault. All the misses will be your friends, and perhaps follow your example. Then you will have the pleasure of having caused the quiet of the whole school; your governess will love you; and you will be at peace in your mind, and never have any more foolish quarrels, in which you all get nothing but blows and uneasiness.

Miss Sukey began now to find, that Miss Jenny was in the right, and she herself in the wrong; but yet she was so proud she would not own it. Nothing could be so foolish as this pride; because it would have been both good and wise in her to confess the truth the moment she saw it. However, Miss Jenny was so discreet as not to press her any farther that night; but begged her to consider seriously on what she had said, and to let her know her thoughts the next morning and then left her.

When Miss Sukey was alone she stood some time in great confusion. She could not help seeing how much hitherto she had been in the wrong; and that thought stung her to the heart. She cried, stamped, and was in as great an agony as if some sad misfortune had befallen her. At last, when she had somewhat vented her passion by tears, she burst forth into the following speech:

'It is very true what Miss Jenny Peace says; for I am always uneasy. I don't sleep in quiet because I am always thinking, either that I have not my share of what is given us, or that I cannot be revenged on any of the girls that offend me. And when I quarrel with them, I am scratched and bruised; or reproached. And what do I get by all this? Why, I scratch, bruise, and reproach them in my turn. Is not that gain enough? I warrant I hurt them as much as they hurt me. But then indeed, as Miss Jenny says, if I could make these girls my friends, and did not wish to hurt them, I certainly might live a quieter, and perhaps a happier, life. But what then, have I been always in the wrong all my lifetime? for I always quarrelled and hated everyone who had offended me. Oh! I cannot bear that thought! It is enough to make me mad! when I imagined myself so wise and so sensible, to find out that I have been always a fool. If I think a moment longer about it, I shall die with grief and shame. I must think myself in the right; and I will too. But, as Miss Jenny says, I really am unhappy; for I hate all my schoolfellows; and yet I dare not do them any mischief; for my mistress will punish me severely if I do. I should not so much mind that neither; but then those I intend to hurt will triumph over me, to see me punished for their sakes. In short, the more I reflect, the more I am afraid Miss Jenny is in the right; and yet it breaks my heart to think so.'

Here the poor girl wept so bitterly, and was so heartily grieved, that she could not utter one word more; but sat herself down, reclining her head upon her hand, in the most melancholy posture that could be; nor could she close her eyes all night, but lay tossing and raving with the thought how she should act, and what she should say to Miss Jenny the next day.

When the morning came, Miss Sukey dreaded every moment, as the time drew nearer when she must meet Miss Jenny. She knew it would not be possible to resist her arguments; and yet shame for having been in fault overcame her.

As soon as Miss Jenny saw Miss Sukey with her eyes cast down, and confessing, by a look of sorrow, that she would take her advice, she embraced her kindly; and, without giving her the trouble to speak, took it for granted, that she would leave off quarreling, be reconciled to her schoolfellows, and make herself happy.

Miss Sukey did indeed stammer out some words, which implied a confession of her fault; but they were spoke so low they could hardly be heard; only Miss Jenny, who always chose to look at the fairest side of her companions' actions, by Miss Sukey's look and manner guessed her meaning.

In the same manner did this good girl, Jenny, persuade, one by one, all her schoolfellows to be reconciled to each with sincerity and love.

Miss Dolly Friendly, who had too much sense to engage the battle for the sake of an apple, and who was provoked to strike a blow only for friendship's sake, easily saw the truth of what Miss Jenny said; and was therefore presently convinced, that the best part she could have acted for her friend, would have been to have withdrawn her from the scuffle.

A SCENE OF LOVE AND FRIENDSHIP, QUITE THE REVERSE OF THE BATTLE,

WHEREIN ARE SHOWN THE DIFFERENT EFFECTS OF LOVE AND GOODNESS FROM THOSE ATTENDING ANGER, STRIFE, AND WICKEDNESS: WITH THE LIFE OF MISS JENNY PEACE.

After Miss Jenny had completed the good work of making all her companions friends, she drew them round her in a little arbour, in that very garden which had been the scene of their strife, and consequently of their misery; and then spoke to them the following speech; which she delivered in so mild a voice, that it was sufficient to charm her hearers into attention, and to persuade them to be led by her advice, and to follow her example in the paths of goodness.

'My dear friends and schoolfellows, you cannot imagine the happiness it gives me to see you thus all so heartily reconciled. You will find the joyful fruits of it. Nothing can show so much sense as thus to own yourselves in fault; for could anything have been so foolish as to spend all your time in misery, rather than at once to make use of the power you have of making yourselves happy? Now if you will use as many endeavours to love as you have hitherto done to hate each other, you will find that every one amongst you, whenever you have anything given you, will have double, nay, I may say eight times (as there are eight of you) the pleasure, in considering that your companions are happy. What is the end of quarrels, but that everyone is fretted and vexed, and no one gains anything! Whereas by endeavouring to please and love each other, the end is happiness to ourselves, and joy to everyone around us. I am sure, if you will speak the truth, none of you have been so easy since you quarrelled, as you are now you are reconciled. Answer me honestly, if this is not truth.'

Here Miss Jenny was silent, and waited for an answer. But the poor girls, who had in them the seeds of goodwill to each other, although those seeds were choked and overrun with the weeds of envy and pride; as in a garden the finest strawberries will be spoiled by rank weeds, if care is not taken to root them out; these poor girls, I say, now struck with the force of truth, and sorry for what they had done, let drop some tears, which trickled down their cheeks, and were signs of meekness, and sorrow for their fault. Not like those tears which burst from their swollen eyes, when anger and hatred choked their words, and their proud hearts laboured with stubbornness and folly; when their skins reddened, and all their features were changed and distorted by the violence of passion, which made them frightful to the beholders, and miserable to themselves;— No! Far other cause had they now for tears, and far different were the tears they shed; their eyes, melted with sorrow for their faults, let fall some drops, as tokens of their repentance; but, as soon as they could recover themselves to speak, they all with one voice cried out, 'Indeed, Miss Jenny, we are sorry for our fault, and will follow your advice; which we now see is owing to your goodness.'

Miss Jenny now produced a basket of apples, which she had purchased out of the little pocket-money she was allowed, in order to prove, that the same things may be a pleasure or a pain, according as the persons to whom they are given are good or bad.

These she placed in the midst of her companions, and desired them to eat, and enjoy themselves; and now they were so changed, that each helped her next neighbour before she would touch any for herself; and the moment they were grown thus good natured and friendly, they were as well-bred, and as polite, as it is possible to describe.

Miss Jenny's joy was inexpressible, that she had caused this happy change; nor less was the joy of her companions, who now began to taste pleasures, from which their animosity to each other had hitherto debarred them. They all sat looking pleased on their companions; their faces borrowed beauty from the calmness and goodness of their minds; and all those ugly frowns, and all that ill-natured sourness, which when they were angry and cross were but too plain in their faces, were now entirely fled; jessamine and honeysuckles surrounded their seats, and played round their heads, of which they gathered nosegays to present each other with. They now enjoyed all the pleasure and happiness that attend those who are innocent and good.

Miss Jenny, with her heart overflowing with joy at this happy change, said, 'Now, my dear companions, that you may be convinced what I have said and done was not occasioned by any desire of proving myself wiser than you, as Miss Sukey hinted while she was yet in her anger, I will, if you please, relate to you the history of my past life; by which you will see in what manner I came by this way of thinking; and as you will perceive it was chiefly owing to the instructions of a kind mamma, you may all likewise reap the same advantage under good Mrs. Teachum, if you will obey her commands, and attend to her precepts. And after I have given you the particulars of my life, I must beg that every one of you will, some day or other, when you have reflected upon it, declare all that you can remember of your own; for, should you not be able to relate anything worth remembering as an example, yet there is nothing more likely to amend the future part of anyone's life, than the recollecting and confessing the faults of the past.'

All our little company highly approved of Miss Jenny's proposal, and promised, in their turns, to relate their own lives; and Miss Polly Suckling cried out, 'Yes indeed, Miss Jenny, I'll tell all when it comes to my turn; so pray begin, for I long to hear what you did, when you was no bigger than I am now.' Miss Jenny then kissed little Polly, and said she would instantly begin.

But as in the reading of any one's story, it is an additional pleasure to have some acquaintance with their persons; and as I delight in giving my little readers every pleasure that is in my power; I shall endeavour, as justly as I can, by description, to set before their eyes the picture of this good young creature: and in the same of every one of our young company, as they begin their lives.

THE DESCRIPTION OF MISS JENNY PEACE.

Miss Jenny Peace was just turned of fourteen, and could be called neither tall nor short of her age; but her whole person was the most agreeable that can be imagined. She had an exceeding fine complexion, with as much colour in her cheeks as is the natural effect of perfect health. Her hair was light brown, and curled in so regular and yet easy a manner, as never to want any assistance from art. Her eyebrows (which were not of that correct turn as to look as if they were drawn with a pencil) and her eyelashes were both darker than her hair; and the latter being very long, gave such a shade to her eyes as made them often mistaken for black, though they were only a dark hazel. To give any description of her eyes beyond the colour and size, which was perfectly the medium, would be impossible; except by saying they were expressive of everything that is amiable and good; for through them might be read every single thought of the mind; from whence they had such a brightness and cheerfulness, as seemed to cast a lustre over her whole face. She had fine teeth, and a mouth answering to the most correct rules of beauty; and when she spoke (though you were at too great a distance to hear what she said) there appeared so much sweetness, mildness, modesty and good nature, that you found yourself filled more with pleasure than admiration in beholding her. The delight which everyone took in looking on Miss Jenny was evident in this, that though Miss Sukey Jennett and Miss Patty Lockit were both what may be called handsomer girls (and if you asked any persons in company their opinion, they would tell you so) yet their eyes were a direct contradiction to their tongues, by being continually fixed on Miss Jenny; for, while she was in the room, it was impossible to fix them anywhere else. She had a natural ease and gentility in her shape; and all her motions were more pleasing, though less striking than what is commonly acquired by the instruction of dancing masters.

Such was the agreeable person of Miss Jenny Peace, who, in her usual obliging manner, and with an air pleasing beyond my power to express, at the request of her companions began to relate the history of her life, as follows:

THE LIFE OF MISS JENNY PEACE.

'My father dying when I was but half a year old, I was left to the care of my mamma, who was the best woman in the world, and to whose memory I shall ever pay the most grateful honour. From the time she had any children, she made it the whole study of her life to promote their welfare, and form their minds in the manner she thought would best answer her purpose of making them both good and happy; for it was her constant maxim, that goodness and happiness dwelt in the same bosoms, and were generally found to life so much together, that they could not easily be separated.

'My mother had six children born alive; but could preserve none beyond the first year, except my brother, Harry Peace, and myself. She made it one of her chief cares to cultivate and preserve the most perfect love and harmony between us. My brother is but a twelvemonth older than I; so that, till I was six years old (for seven was the age in which he was sent to school) he remained at home with me; in which time we often had little childish quarrels; but my mother always took care to convince us of our error in wrangling and fighting about nothing, and to teach us how much more pleasure we enjoyed whilst we agreed. She showed no partiality to either, but endeavoured to make us equal in all things, any otherwise than that she taught me I owed a respect to my brother as the eldest.

'Before my brother went to school, we had set hours appointed us, in which we regularly attended to learn whatever was thought necessary for our improvement; my mamma herself daily watching the opening of our minds, and taking great care to instruct us in what manner to make the best use of the knowledge we attained. Whatever we read she explained to us, and made us understand, that we might be the better for our lessons. When we were capable of thinking, we made it so much a rule to obey our parent, the moment she signified her pleasure, that by that means we avoided many accidents and misfortunes; for example: my brother was running one day giddily round the brink of a well; and if he had made the least false step, he must have fallen to the bottom, and been drowned; my mamma, by a sign with her finger that called him to her, preserved him from the imminent danger he was in of losing his life; and then she took care that we should both be the better for this little incident, by laying before us how much our safety and happiness, as well as our duty, were concerned in being obedient.

'My brother and I once had a quarrel about something as trifling as your apple of contention; and, though we both heartily wished to be reconciled to each other, yet did our little hearts swell so much with stubbornness and pride, that neither of us would speak first; by which means we were so silly as to be both uneasy, and yet would not use the remedy that was in our own power to remove that uneasiness. My mamma found it out, and sent for me into her closet, and said, "She was sorry to see her instructions had no better effect on me; for," continued she, "indeed, Jenny, I am ashamed of your folly, as well as wickedness, in thus contending with your brother." A tear, which I believe flowed from shame, started from my eyes at this reproof; and I fixed them on the ground, being too much overwhelmed with confusion to dare to lift them up on mamma. On which she kindly said, "She hoped my confusion was a sign of my amendment. That she might indeed have used another method, by commanding me to seek a reconciliation with my brother; for she did not imagine I was already so far gone in perverseness, as not to hold her commands as inviolable; but she was willing, for my good, first to convince me of my folly." As soon as my confusion would give me leave to speak, on my knees I gave her a thousand thanks for her goodness, and went immediately to seek my brother. He joyfully embraced the first opportunity of being reconciled to me; and this was one of the pleasantest hours of my life. This quarrel happened when my brother came home at a breaking-up, and I was nine years old.

'My mamma's principal care was to keep up a perfect amity between me and my brother. I remember once, when Harry and I were playing in the fields, there was a small rivulet stopped me in my way. My brother, being nimbler and better able to jump than myself, with one spring leaped over, and left me on the other side of it; but seeing me uneasy that I could not get over to him, his good nature prompted him to come back and to assist me; and, by the help of his hand, I easily passed over. On this my good mamma bid me remember how much my brother's superior strength might assist me in his being my protector; and that I ought to return to use my utmost endeavours to oblige him; and that then we should be mutual assistants to each other throughout life. Thus everything that passed was made use of to improve my understanding and amend my heart.

'I believe no child ever spent her time more agreeably than I did; for I not only enjoyed my own pleasures, but also those of others. And when my brother was carried abroad, and I was left at home, that HE was pleased, made me full amends for the loss of any diversion, the contentions between us (where our parent's commands did not interfere) were always exerted in endeavours each to prefer the other's pleasures to our own. My mind was easy and free from anxiety; for as I always took care to speak truth, I had nothing to conceal from my mamma, and consequently had never any fears of being found in a lie. For one lie obliges us to tell a thousand others to conceal it; and I have no notion of any conditions being so miserable, as to live in a continual fear of detection. Most particularly, my mamma instructed me to beware of all sorts of deceit; so that I was accustomed, not only in words to speak truth, but also not to endeavour by any means to deceive.

'But though the friendship between my brother and me was so strongly cultivated, yet we were taught, that lying for each other, or praising each other when it was not deserved, was not only a fault, but a very great crime; for this, my mamma used to tell us, was not love, but hatred; as it was encouraging one another in folly and wickedness. And though my natural disposition inclined me to be very tender of everything in my power, yet was I not suffered to give way even to THIS in an unreasonable degree. One instance of which I remember.

'When I was about eleven years old, I had a cat that I had bred up from a little kitten, that used to play round me, till I had indulged for the poor animal a fondness that made me delight to have it continually with me wherever I went; and, in return for my indulgence, the cat seemed to have changed its nature, and assumed the manner that more properly belongs to dogs than cats; for it would follow me about the house and gardens, mourn for my absence, and rejoice at my presence. And, what was very remarkable, the poor animal would, when fed by my hand, lose that caution which cats are known to be possessed of, and eat whatever I gave it, as if it could reflect that I meant only its good, and no harm could come from me.

'I was at last so accustomed to see this little Frisk (for so I called it) playing round me, that I seemed to miss part of myself in its absence. But one day the poor little creature followed me to the door; when a parcel of schoolboys coming by, one of them catched her up in his arms, and ran away with her. All my cries were to no purpose; for he was out of sight with her in a moment, and there was no method to trace his steps. The cruel wretches, for sport, as they called it, hunted it the next day from one to the other, in the most barbarous manner; till at last it took shelter in that house that used to be its protection, and came and expired at my feet.

'I was so struck with the sight of the little animal dying in that manner, that the great grief of my heart overflowed at my eyes, and I was for some time inconsolable.

'My indulgent mamma comforted without blaming me, till she thought I had sufficient time to vent my grief; and then, sending for me into her chamber, spoke as follows:

'"Jenny, I have watched you ever since the death of your little favourite cat; and have been in hopes daily, that your lamenting and melancholy on that account would be at an end. But I find you still persist in grieving, as if such a loss was irreparable. Now, though I have always encouraged you in all sentiments of good nature and compassion; and am sensible, that where those sentiments are strongly implanted, they will extend their influence even to the least animal; yet you are to consider, my child, that you are not to give way to any passions that interfere with your duty; for whenever there is any contention between your duty and your inclinations, you must conquer the latter, or become wicked and contemptible. If, therefore, you give way to this melancholy, how will you be able to perform your duty towards me, in cheerfully obeying my commands, and endeavouring, by your lively prattle and innocent gaiety of heart, to be my companion and delight? Nor will you be fit to converse with your brother, whom (as you lost your good papa when you were too young to know that loss) I have endeavoured to educate in such a manner, that I hope he will be a father to you, if you deserve his love and protection. In short, if you do not keep command enough of yourself to prevent being ruffled by every accident, you will be unfit for all the social offices of life, and be despised by all those whose regard and love are worth your seeking. I treat you, my girl, as capable of considering what is for your own good; for though you are but eleven years of age, yet I hope the pains I have taken in explaining all you read, and in answering all your questions in search of knowledge, has not been so much thrown away, but that you are more capable of judging, than those unhappy children are, whose parents have neglected to instruct them. And therefore, farther to enforce what I say, remember, that repining at any accident that happens to you, is an offence to that God to whom I have taught you daily to pray for all the blessings you can receive, and to whom you are to return humble thanks for every blessing."

'"I expect therefore, Jenny, that you now dry up your tears, and resume your usual cheerfulness. I do not doubt but your obedience to me will make you at least put on the appearance of cheerfulness in my sight. But you will deceive yourself, if you think that is performing your duty; for if you would obey me as you ought, you must try heartily to root from your mind all sorrow and gloominess. You may depend upon it, this command is in your power to obey; for you know I never require anything of you that is impossible."

'After my mamma had made this speech, she went out to take a walk in the garden, and left me to consider of what she had said.

'The moment I came to reflect seriously, I found it was indeed in my power to root all melancholy from my heart, when I considered it was necessary, in order to perform my duty to God, to obey the best of mothers, and to make myself a blessing and a cheerful companion to her, rather than a burden, and the cause of her uneasiness, by my foolish melancholy.

'This little accident, as managed by my mamma, has been a lesson to me in governing my passions ever since.

'It would be endless to repeat all the methods this good mother invented for my instruction, amendment, and improvement. It is sufficient to acquaint you, that she contrived that every new day should open to me some new scene of knowledge; and no girl could be happier than I was during her life. But, alas! when I was thirteen years of age, the scene changed. My dear mamma was taken ill of a scarlet fever. I attended her day and night whilst she lay ill, my eyes starting with tears to see her in that condition; and yet I did not dare to give my sorrows vent, for fear of increasing her pain.'

Here a trickling tear stole from Miss Jenny's eyes. She suppressed some rising sobs that interrupted her speech, and was about to proceed in her story, when, casting her eyes on her companions, she saw her sorrow had such an effect upon them all, that there was not one of her hearers who could refrain from shedding a sympathising tear. She therefore thought it was more strictly following her mamma's precepts to pass this part of her story in silence, rather than to grieve her friends; and having wiped away her tears, she hastened to conclude her story; which she did as follows:

'After my mamma's death, my Aunt Newman, my father's sister, took the care of me; but being obliged to go to Jamaica, to settle some affairs relating to an estate she is possessed of there, she took with her my Cousin Harriet, her only daughter, and left me under the care of the good Mrs. Teachum till her return. And since I have been here, you all know as much of my history as I do myself.'

As Miss Jenny spoke these words, the bell summoned them to supper into the presence of their governess, who having narrowly watched their looks ever since the fray, had hitherto plainly perceived, that though they did not dare to break out again into an open quarrel, yet their hearts had still harboured unkind thoughts of one another. She was surprised NOW, as she stood at a window in the hall that overlooked the garden, to see all her scholars walk towards her hand in hand, with such cheerful countenances, as plainly showed their inward good humour. And as she thought proper to mention to them her pleasure in seeing them thus altered, Miss Jenny Peace related to her governess all that had passed in the arbour, with their general reconciliation. Mrs. Teachum gave Miss Jenny all the applause due to her goodness, saying, she herself had only waited a little while, to see if their anger would subside, and love take its place in their bosoms, without her interfering again; for THAT she certainly should otherwise have done, to have brought about what Miss Jenny had so happily effected.

Miss Jenny thanked her governess for her kind approbation, and said, that if she would give them leave, she would spend what time she was pleased to allow them from school in this little arbour, in reading stories, and such things as she should think a proper and innocent amusement.

Mrs. Teachum not only gave leave, but very much approved of this proposal; and desired Miss Jenny, as a reward for what she had already done, to preside over these diversions, and to give her an account in what manner they proceeded. Miss Jenny promised in all things to be guided by good Mrs. Teachum. And now, soon after supper, they retired to rest, free from those uneasy passions which used to prevent their quiet; and as they had passed the day in pleasure, at night they sunk in soft and sweet repose.

MONDAY.

THE FIRST DAY AFTER THEIR REPENTANCE; AND, CONSEQUENTLY, THE FIRST DAY OF THE HAPPINESS OF MISS JENNY PEACE AND HER COMPANIONS.

Early in the morning, as soon as Miss Jenny arose, all her companions flocked round her; for they now looked on her as the best friend they had in the world; and they agreed, when they came out of school, to adjourn into their arbour, and divert themselves till dinner-time; which they accordingly did. When Miss Jenny proposed, if it was agreeable to them to hear it, to read them a story which she had put in her pocket for that purpose; and as they now began to look upon her as the most proper person to direct them in their amusements, they all replied, What was most agreeable to her would please them best. She then began to read the following story, with which we shall open their first day's amusement.

THE STORY OF THE CRUEL GIANT BARBARICO, THE GOOD GIANT BENEFICO,
AND THE LITTLE PRETTY DWARF MIGNON.

A great many hundred years ago, the mountains of Wales were inhabited by two giants; one of whom was the terror of all his neighbours and the plague of the whole country. He greatly exceeded the size of any giant recorded in history; and his eyes looked so fierce and terrible, that they frightened all who were so unhappy as to behold them.

The name of this enormous wretch was Barbarico. A name which filled all who heard it with fear and astonishment. The whole delight of this monster's life was in acts of inhumanity and mischief; and he was the most miserable as well as the most wicked creature that ever yet was born. He had no sooner committed one outrage, but he was in agonies till he could commit another; never satisfied, unless he could find an opportunity of either torturing or devouring some innocent creature. And whenever he happened to be disappointed in any of his malicious purposes, he would stretch his immense bulk on the top of some high mountain, and groan, and beat the earth, and bellow with such a hollow voice, that the whole country heard and trembled at the sound.

The other giant, whose name was Benefico, was not so tall and bulky as the hideous Barbarico. He was handsome, well proportioned, and of a very good-natured turn of mind. His delight was no less in acts of goodness and benevolence than the other's was in cruelty and mischief. His constant care was to endeavour if possible to repair the injuries committed by this horrid tyrant, which he had sometimes an opportunity of doing; for though Barbarico was much larger and stronger than Benefico, yet his coward mind was afraid to engage with him, and always shunned a meeting; leaving the pursuit of any prey, if he himself was pursued by Benefico: nor could the good Benefico trust farther to this coward spirit of his base adversary, than only to make the horrid creature fly; for he well knew that a close engagement might make him desperate; and fatal to himself might be the consequence of such a brutal desperation; therefore he prudently declined any attempt to destroy this cruel monster, till he should gain some sure advantage over him.

It happened on a certain day, that as the inhuman Barbarico was prowling along the side of a craggy mountain overgrown with brambles and briery thickets, taking most horrid strides, rolling his ghastly eyes around in quest of human blood, and having his breast tortured with inward rage and grief, that he had been so unhappy as to live one whole day without some act of violence, he beheld, in a pleasant valley at a distance, a little rivulet winding its gentle course through rows of willows mixed with flowery shrubs. Hither the giant hasted; and being arrived, he gazed about to see if in this sweet retirement any were so unhappy as to fall within his power; but finding none, the disappointment set him in a flame of rage, which, burning like an inward furnace, parched his throat. And now he laid him down on the bank, to try if in the cool stream, that murmured as it flowed, he could assuage or slack the fiery thirst that burnt within him.

He bent him down to drink; and at the same time casting his baleful eyes towards the opposite side, he discovered within a little natural arbour formed by the branches of a spreading tree, within the meadow's flowery lawn, the shepherd Fidus and his loved Amata.

The gloomy tyrant no sooner perceived this happy pair, than his heart exulted with joy; and, suddenly leaping up on the ground, he forgot his thirst, and left the stream untasted. He stood for a short space to view them in their sweet retirement; and was soon convinced that, in the innocent enjoyment of reciprocal affection, their happiness was complete. His eyes, inflamed with envy to behold such bliss, darted a fearful glare; and his breast swelling with malice and envenomed rage, he with gigantic pace approached their peaceful seat.

The happy Fidus was at that time busy in entertaining his loved Amata with a song which he had that very morning composed in praise of constancy; and the giant was now within one stride of them, when Amata, perceiving him, cried out in a trembling voice, 'Fly, Fidus, fly, or we are lost for ever; we are pursued by the hateful Barbarico!' She had scarce uttered these words, when the savage tyrant seized them by the waist in either hand, and holding up to his nearer view, thus said: 'Speak, miscreants; and, if you would avoid immediate death, tell me who you are, and whence arises that tranquility of mind, which even at a distance was visible in your behaviour.'

Poor Fidus, with looks that would have melted the hardest heart, innocently replied, that they were wandering that way without designing offence to any creature on earth. That they were faithful lovers; and, with the consent of all their friends and relations, were soon to be married; therefore he entreated him not to part them.

The giant now no sooner perceived, from the last words of the affrighted youth, what was most likely to give him the greatest torment, than with a spiteful grin which made his horrible face yet more horrible, and in a hollow voice, as loud as thunder, he tauntingly cried out, 'Ho-hoh! You'd not be parted, would you? For once I'll gratify thy will, and thou shalt follow this thy whimpering fondling down my capatious maw.' So saying, he turned his ghastly visage on the trembling Amata who, being now no longer able to support herself under his cruel threats, fainted away, and remained in his hand but as a lifeless corpse. When lifting up his eyes towards the hill on the opposite side, he beheld Benefico coming hastily towards him. This good giant having been that morning informed that Barbarico was roaming in the mountains after prey, left his peaceful castle, in hopes of giving protection to whatever unfortunate creature should fall into the clutches of this so cruel a monster.

Barbarico, at the sight of the friendly Benefico, started with fear; for although in bulk and stature he was, as we have said, the superior: yet that cowardice, which ever accompanies wickedness, now wrought in him in such a manner that he could not bear to confront him, well knowing the courage and fortitude that always attend the good and virtuous; and therefore instantly putting Fidus into the wallet that hung over his shoulder, he flung the fainting Amata, whom he took to be quite expired, into the stream that ran hard by, and fled to his cave, not daring once to cast his eyes behind him.

The good Benefico perceiving the monster's flight, and not doubting but he had been perpetrating some horrid mischief, immediately hastened to the brook; where he found the half-expiring Amata floating down the stream, for her clothes had yet borne her up on the surface of the water. He speedily stepped in and drew her out, and taking her in his arms, pressed her to his warm bosom; and in a short space perceiving in her face the visible marks of returning life, his heart swelled with kind compassion, and he thus bespoke the tender maid: 'Unhappy damsel, lift up thy gentle eyes, and tell me by what hard fate thou hast fallen into the power of that barbarous monster, whose savage nature delights in nothing but ruin and desolation. Tremble not thus, but without fear or terror behold one who joys in the thought of having saved thee from destruction, and will bring thee every comfort his utmost power can procure.'

The gentle Amata was now just enough recovered to open her eyes: but finding herself in a giant's arms, and still retaining in her mind the frightful image of the horrid Barbarico, she fetched a deep sigh, crying out in broken accents, 'Fly, Fidus, fly;' and again sunk down upon the friendly giant's breast. On hearing these words, and plainly seeing by the anguish of her mind that some settled grief was deeply rooted at her heart, and therefore despairing to bring her to herself immediately, the kind Benefico hastened with her to his hospitable castle; where every imaginable assistance was administered to her relief, in order to recover her lost sense, and to reconcile her to her wretched fate.

The cruel Barbarico was no sooner arrived at his gloomy cave, than he called to him his little page; who, trembling to hear the tyrant now again returned, quickly drew near to attend his stern commands: when drawing out of the wallet the poor Fidus, more dead than alive, the monster cried out, 'Here, caitiff, take in charge this smoothed-faced miscreant; and, d'ye hear me? see that his allowance be no more than one small ounce of mouldy bread and half a pint of standing water, for each day's support, till his now blooming skin be withered, his flesh be wasted from his bones, and he dwindle to a meagre skeleton.' So saying he left them, as he hoped, to bewail each other's sad condition. But the unhappy Fidus, bereft of his Amata, was not to be appalled by any of the most horrid threats; for now his only comfort was the hopes of a speedy end to his miserable life, and to find a refuge from his misfortunes in the peaceful grave. With this reflection the faithful Fidus was endeavouring to calm the inward troubles of his mind, when the little page, with looks of the most tender compassion, and in gentle words, bid him be comforted, and with patience endure his present affliction; adding that he himself had long suffered the most rigorous fate, yet despaired not but that one day would give them an opportunity to free themselves from the wicked wretch, whose sole delight was in others' torments. 'As to his inhuman commands,' continued he, 'I will sooner die than obey them; and in a mutual friendship perhaps we may find some consolation, even in this dismal cave.'

This little page the cruel Barbarico had stolen from his parents at five years old; ever since which time he had tortured and abused him, till he had now attained the age of one-and-twenty. His mother had given him the name of Mignon; by which name the monster always called him, as it gratified his insolence to make use of that fond appellation whilst he was abusing him, only when he said Mignon he would in derision add the word Dwarf; for, to say the truth, Mignon was one of the least men that was ever seen, though at the same time one of the prettiest: his limbs, though small, were exactly proportioned; his countenance was at once sprightly and soft; and whatever his head thought, or his heart felt, his eyes by their looks expressed; and his temper was as sweet as his person was amiable. Such was the gentle creature Barbarico chose to torment. For wicked giants, no less than wicked men and women, are constantly tormented at the appearance of those perfections in another, to which they themselves have no pretensions.

The friendship and affection of Fidus and Mignon now every day increased; and the longer they were acquainted, the mere delight they took in each other's company. The faithful Fidus related to his companion the story of his loved Amata, whilst the tender Mignon consoled his friend's inward sorrows, and supplied him with necessaries, notwithstanding the venture he run of the cruel tyrant's heavy displeasure. The giant ceased not every day to view the hapless Fidus, to see if the cruelty of his intentions had in any degree wrought its desired effect; but perceiving in him no alteration, he now began to be suspicious that the little Mignon had not punctually obeyed his savage command. In order therefore to satisfy his wicked curiosity, he resolved within himself narrowly to watch every occasion these poor unhappy captives had of conversing with each other. Mignon, well knowing the implacable and revengeful disposition of this barbarous tyrant, had taken all the precautions imaginable to avoid discovery; and therefore generally sought every opportunity of being alone with Fidus, and carrying him his daily provisions at those hours he knew the giant was most likely to be asleep.

It so befell that, on a certain day, the wicked giant had, as was his usual custom, been abroad for many hours in search of some unhappy creature on whom to glut his hateful inhumanity; when, tired with fruitless roaming, he returned to his gloomy cave, beguiled of all his horrid purposes; for he had not once that day espied so much as the track of man, or other harmless animal, to give him hopes even to gratify his rage or cruelty; but now raving with inward torment and despair, he laid him down upon his iron couch, to try if he could close his eyes and quiet the tumultuous passions of his breast. He tossed and tumbled and could get no rest, starting with fearful dreams, and horrid visions of tormenting furies.

Meanwhile the gentle Mignon had prepared a little delicate repast, and having seen the monster lay himself at length, and thinking now that a fit occasion offered in which to comfort and refresh his long-expecting friend, was hastening with it to the cell where the faithful Fidus was confined. At the fatal moment the giant, rearing himself up on his couch, perceived the little Mignon just at the entrance of the cell; when calling to him in a hollow voice, that dismally resounded through the cave, he so startled the poor unhappy page, that he dropped the cover from his trembling hand and stood fixed and motionless as a statue.

'Come hither, Mignon, caitiff, dwarf,' said then the taunting homicide: but the poor little creature was so thunderstruck he was quite unable to stir one foot. Whereat the giant, rousing himself from off his couch, with one huge stride reached out his brawny arm, and seized him by the waist; and, pointing to the scattered delicates, cried out, 'Vile miscreant! is it thus thou hast obeyed my orders? Is this the mouldy bread and muddy water, with which alone it was my command thou shouldst sustain that puny mortal? But I'll—' Here raising him aloft, he was about to dash him to the ground, when suddenly revolving in his wicked thoughts, that if at once he should destroy his patient slave, his cruelty to him must also have an end, he paused—and then recovering, he stretched out his arm, and bringing the little trembler near his glaring eyes, he thus subjoins: 'No; I'll not destroy thy wretched life; but thou shalt waste thy weary days in a dark dungeon, as far remote from the least dawn of light as from thy loved companion. And I myself will carefully supply you both so equally with mouldy bread and water, that each by his own sufferings shall daily know what his dear friend endures.' So saying, he hastened with him to his deepest dungeon; and having thrust him in, he doubly barred the iron door. And now again retiring to his couch, this new-wrought mischief, which greatly gratified his raging mind, soon sunk him down into a sound and heavy sleep. The reason this horrid monster had not long ago devoured his little captive (for he thought him a delicious morsel) was, that he might never want an object at hand to gratify his cruelty. For though extremely great was his voracious hunger, yet greater still was his desire of tormenting; and oftentimes when he had teased, beat, and tortured the poor gentle Mignon, so as to force from him tears, and sometimes a soft complaint, he would, with a malicious sneer, scornfully reproach him in the following words: 'Little does it avail to whine, to blubber, or complain; for, remember, abject wretch,

I am a giant, and I can eat thee: Thou art a dwarf, and thou canst not eat me.'

When Mignon was thus alone, he threw himself on the cold ground, bemoaning his unhappy fate. However, he soon recollected that patience and resignation were his only succour in this distressful condition; not doubting but that, as goodness cannot always suffer, he should in time meet with some unforeseen deliverance from the savage power of the inhuman Barbarico.

Whilst the gentle Mignon was endeavouring to comfort himself in his dungeon with these good reflections, he suddenly perceived, at a little distance from him, a small glimmering light. Immediately he rose from the ground, and going towards it, found that it shone through a little door that had been left at jar, which led him to a spacious hall, wherein the giant hoarded his immense treasures. Mignon was at first dazzled with the lustre of so much gold and silver, and sparkling jewels as were there heaped together. But casting his eyes on a statue that was placed in the middle of the room, he read on the pedestal, written in very small letters, the following verses:

Wouldst thou from the rage be free   Of the tyrant's tyranny,   Loose the fillet which is bound   Twice three times my brows around;   Bolts and bars shall open fly,   By a magic sympathy. Take him in his sleeping hour;   Bind his neck and break his pow'r.   Patience bids, make no delay: Haste to bind him, haste away.

Mignon's little heart now leapt for joy, that he had found the means of such a speedy deliverance; and eagerly climbing up the statue, he quickly unbound the magic fillet; which was no sooner done, but suddenly the bolts and bars of the brazen gates through which the giant used to pass to this his treasury, were all unloosed, and the folding-doors of their own accord flew open, grating harsh thunder on their massy hinges. At the same instant, stretched on his iron couch in the room adjoining to the hall, the giant gave a deadly groan. Here again the little Mignon's trembling heart began to fail; for he feared the monster was awakened by the noise, and that he should now suffer the cruellest torments his wicked malice could invent. Wherefore for a short space he remained clinging round the statue, till he perceived that all again was hushed and silent; when, getting down, he gently stole into the giant's chamber, where he found him still in a profound sleep.

But here, to the great mortification of Miss Jenny's attentive hearers, the hour of entertaining themselves being at an end, they were obliged to leave the poor little Mignon in the greatest distress and fright lest the giant should awake before he could fulfil the commands of the oracle, and to wait for the remainder of the story till another opportunity.

In the evening, as soon as school was over, the little company again met in their arbour, and nothing could be greater than their impatience to hear the event of Mignon's hazardous undertaking. Miss Dolly Friendly said that if the poor little creature was destroyed, she should not sleep that night. But they all joined in entreating Miss Jenny to proceed; which she did in the following manner:

A CONTINUATION OF THE STORY OF THE GIANTS.

Now, thought Mignon, is the lucky moment to fulfil the instructions of the oracle. And then cautiously getting up the side of the couch, with trembling hands he put the fillet round the monster's neck, and tied it firmly in a threefold knot; and again softly creeping down, he retired into a corner of the room to wait the wished event. In a few minutes the giant waked; and opening his enormous eyes, he glared their horrid orbs around (but without the least motion of his head or body) and spied the little Mignon where he lay, close shrinking to avoid his baleful sight.

The giant no sooner perceived his little page at liberty, but his heart sorely smote him, and he began to suspect the worst that could befall; for, recollecting that he had carelessly left open the little door leading from the dungeon to the great hall wherein was placed the fatal magic statue, he was now entirely convinced that Mignon had discovered the secret charm on which his power depended; for he already found the magic of the fillet round his neck fully to operate, his sinews all relax, his joints all tremble; and when he would by his own hand have tried to free himself, his shivering limbs he found refused obedience to their office. Thus bereft of all his strength, and well nigh motionless, in this extremity of impotence he cast about within himself by what sly fraud and subtlety were now his only refuge) he best might work upon the gentle Mignon to lend his kind assistance to unloose him. Wherefore with guileful words and seeming courtesy, still striving to conceal his cursed condition, he thus bespake his little captive:

'Come hither Mignon; my pretty gentle boy, come near me. This fillet thou has bound around my neck, to keep me from the cold, gives me some pain. I know thy gentle nature will not let thee see thy tender master in the least uneasiness, without affording him thy cheerful aid and kind relief. Come hither, my dear child, I say, and loose the knot which in thy kind concern (I thank thee for thy care) thou hast tied so hard, it somewhat frets my neck.'

These words the insidious wretch uttered in such a low trembling tone of voice, and with such an affectation of tenderness, that the little page, who had never before experience from him any such kind of dialect, and but too well knew his savage nature to believe that anything but guile or want of power could move him to the least friendly speech, or kind affection, began now strongly to be persuaded that all was as he wished, and that the power of the inhuman tyrant was at an end. He knew full well, that if the giant had not lost the ability of rising from the couch, he should ere now too sensibly have felt the sad effects of his malicious resentment, and therefore boldly adventured to approach him, and coming near the couch, and finding not the least effort in the monster to reach him, and from thence quite satisfied of the giant's total incapacity of doing farther mischief, he flew with raptures to the cell where Fidus lay confined.

Poor Fidus all this time was quite disconsolate; nor could he guess the cause why his little friend so long had kept away; one while he thought the giant's stern commands had streightened him of all subsistence; another while his heart misgave him for his gentle friend, lest unawares his kind beneficence towards him had caused him to fall a sacrifice to the tyrant's cruel resentment. With these and many other like reflections the unhappy youth was busied, when Mignon, suddenly unbarred the cell, flew to his friend, and eagerly embraced him, cried out, 'Come Fidus, haste, my dearest friend; for thou and all of us are from this moment free. Come and behold the cruel monster, where he lies, bereft of all his strength. I cannot stay to tell thee now the cause; but haste, and thou shall see the dreadful tyrant stretched on his iron couch, deprived of all his wicked power. But first let us unbar each cell, wherein is pent some wretched captive, that we may share a general transport for this our glad deliverance.'

The faithful Fidus, whose heart had known but little joy since he had lost his loved Amata, now felt a dawning hope that he might once more chance to find her, if she had survived their fatal separation; and, without one word of answer, he followed Mignon to the several cells, and soon released all the astonished captives.

Mignon first carried them to behold their former terror, now, to appearance, almost a lifeless corpse; who on seeing them all surround his couch, gave a most hideous roar, which made them tremble, all but the gentle Mignon, who was convinced of the impotence of his rage, and begged them to give him their attendance in the hall; where they were no sooner assembled than he showed them the statue, read them the oracle, and told them every circumstance before related.

They now began to bethink themselves of what method was to be taken to procure their entire liberty; for the influence of the magic fillet extended only to the gates of the hall; and still they remained imprisoned within the dismal cave; and though they knew from the oracle, as well as from what appeared, that the monster's power was at an end, yet still were they to seek the means of their escape from this his horrid abode. At length Mignon again ascended the couch to find the massy key, and spying one end of it peep out from under the pillow, he called to Fidus, who first stepped up to his friend's assistance; the rest by his example quickly followed; and now, by their united force, they dragged the ponderous key from under the monster's head; and then descending they all went to the outer door of the cave, where, with some difficulty, they set wide open the folding iron gates.

They now determined to dispatch a messenger to the good Benefico with the news, which they knew would be so welcome to him and all his guests, and with one voice agreed that Fidus should bear the joyful tidings; and then returned to observe the monster, and to wait the coming of Benefico. The nimble Fidus soon reached the giant's dwelling, where, at a little distance from the castle, he met the good Benefico with a train of happy friends, enjoying the pleasures of the evening, and the instructive and cheerful conversation of their kind protector. Fidus briefly told his errand; and instantly Benefico, with all his train, joyfully hastened to behold the wonders he had related; for now many hearts leapt for joy, in hopes of meeting some friend of whom they had been bereft by the cruelty of the savage Barbarico.

They were not long before they arrived at the horrid cave, where Benefico, proceeding directly to the monster's chamber, suddenly appeared to him at the side of his couch. Barbarico, on seeing him, gave a hideous yell, and rolled his glaring eyes in such a manner as expressed the height of rage and envious bitterness.

Benefico, turning to all the company present, thus spoke, 'How shall I enough praise and admire the gentle Mignon for having put in my power to justice on this execrable wretch, and freeing you all from an insufferable slavery, and the whole country from their terror?' Then reaching the monster's own sword, which hung over his couch, his hand yet suspended over the impious tyrant, he thus said, 'Speak, wretch, if yet the power of speech is left thee; and with thy latest breath declare, what advantage hast thou found of all thy wicked life?'

Barbarico well knew that too bad had been that life, to leave the least room for hope of mercy; and therefore, instead of an answer, he gave another hideous yell, gnashing his horrid teeth, and again rolling his ghastly eyes on all around.

Benefico seeing him thus impenitent and sullen, lifted on high the mighty sword, and with one blow severed his odious head from his enormous body.

The whole assembly gave a shout for joy; and Benefico holding in his hand the monster's yet grinning head, thus addressed his half-astonished companions: 'See here, my friends, the proper conclusion of a rapacious cruel life. But let us hasten from this monster's gloomy cave; and on the top of one of our highest mountains, fixed on a pole, will I set up this joyful spectacle, that all the country round may know themselves at liberty to pursue their rural business or amusements, without the dread of any annoyance from a devouring vile tormentor. And when his treasures, which justly all belong to the good patient Mignon, are removed, we will shut up the mouth of this abominable dwelling; and, casting on the door a heap of earth, we'll hope, in time, that both place and remembrance of this cruel savage may in time be lost.'

Every one readily cried out, that to Benefico, the good Benefico, alone belonged the tyrant's treasures; that Benefico should ever be, as heretofore, their governor, their father, and their kind protector.

The beneficent heart of the good giant was quite melted with this their kind confidence and dependence upon him, and assured them, he should ever regard them as his children: and now, exulting in the general joy that must attend the destruction of this savage monster, when the whole country should find themselves freed from the terror his rapine and desolation, he sent before to his castle, to give intelligence to all within that happy place of the grim monster's fall, and little Mignon's triumph; giving in charge to the harbinger of these tidings, that it should be his first and chiefest care to glad the gentle bosom of a fair disconsolate (who kept herself retired and pent up within her own apartment) with the knowledge that the inhuman monster was no more; and that henceforth sweet peace and rural innocence might reign in all their woods and groves. The hearts of all within the castle bounded with joy, on hearing the report of the inhuman monster's death, and the deliverance of all his captives, and with speedy steps they hastened to meet their kind protector; nor did the melancholy fair one, lest she should seem unthankful for the general blessing, refuse to join the train.

It was not long after the messenger that Benefico, and those his joyful friends, arrived: but the faithful Fidus alone, of all this happy company, was tortured with the inward pangs of a sad grief he could not conquer, and his fond heart remained still captivated to a melting sorrow: nor could even the tender friendship of the gentle Mignon quite remove, though it alleviated, his sadness; but the thoughts of his loved lost amata embittered every joy, and overwhelmed his generous soul with sorrow.

When the company from the castle joined Benefico, he declared to them in what manner their deliverance was effected; and, as a general shout of joy resounded through the neighbouring mountains, Fidus, lifting up his eyes, beheld in the midst of the multitude, standing in a pensive posture, the fair disconsolate. Her tender heart was at the instant overflowing in soft tears, caused by a kind participation of their present transport, yet mixed with the deep sad impression of a grief her bosom was full fraught with. Her face, at first, was almost hid by her white handkerchief, with which she wiped away the trickling drops, which falling, had bedewed her beauteous cheeks: but as she turned her lovely face to view the joyful conquerors, and to speak a welcome to her kind protector, what words can speak the raptures, the astonishment, that swelled the bosom of the faithful youth, when in this fair disconsolate he saw his loved, his constant, his long-lost Amata! Their delighted eyes in the same instant beheld each other, and, breaking on each side from their astonished friends, they flew like lightning into each other's arms.

After they had given a short account of what had passed in their separation, Fidus presented to his loved Amata the kind, the gentle Mignon, with lavish praises of his generous friendship, and steady resolution, in hazarding his life by disobeying the injunctions of the cruel tyrant. No sooner had Amata heard the name of Mignon, but she cried out, 'Surely my happiness is now complete, and all my sorrows, by this joyful moment, are more than fully recompensed; for, in the kind preserver of my Fidus, I have found my brother. My mother lost her little Mignon when he was five years old; and pining grief, after some years vain search, ended her wretched life.'

The generous hearts of all who were present shared the raptures of the faithful Fidus, the lovely Amata, and gentle Mignon, on this happy discovery; and in the warmest congratulations they expressed their joy.

Benefico now led all the delighted company into his castle, where freedom was publicly proclaimed; and every one was left a liberty either to remain there with Benefico, or, loaded with wealth sufficient for their use, to go where their attachments or inclinations might invite them.

Fidus, Amata, and the little Mignon, hesitated not one moment to declare their choice of staying with the generous Benefico.

The nuptials of the faithful Fidus, and his loved Amata, were solemnized in the presence of all their friends.

Benefico passed the remainder of his days in pleasing reflections on his well-spent life.

The treasures of the dead tyrant were turned into blessings by the use they were now made of: little Mignon was loved and cherished by all his companions. Peace, harmony and love reigned in every bosom; dissension, discord, and hatred were banished from this friendly dwelling; and that happiness, which is the natural consequence of goodness, appeared in every cheerful countenance throughout the castle of the good Benefico; and as heretofore affright and terror spread itself from the monster's hateful cave, so now from this peaceful castle was diffused tranquility and joy through all the happy country round.

Thus ended the story of the two giants: and Miss Jenny being tired with reading, they left the arbour for that night, and agreed to meet there again the next day.

As soon as they had supped, Mrs. Teachum sent for Miss Jenny Peace into her closet, and desired an exact account from her of this their first day's amusement, that she might judge from thence how far they might be trusted with the liberty she had given them.

Miss Jenny showed her governess the story she had read; and said, 'I hope, madam, you will not think it an improper one; for it was given me by my mamma; and she told me, that she thought it contained a very excellent moral.'

Mrs. Teachum, having looked it over, thus spoke: 'I have no objection, Miss Jenny, to your reading any stories to amuse you, provided you read them with the proper disposition of mind not to be hurt by them. A very good moral may indeed be drawn from the whole, and likewise from almost every part of it; and as you had this story from your mamma, I doubt not but you are very well qualified to make the proper remarks yourself upon the moral of it to your companions. But here let me observe to you (which I would have you communicate to your little friends) that giants, magic, fairies, and all sorts of supernatural assistances in a story, are only introduced to amuse and divert: for a giant is called so only to express a man of great power; and the magic fillet round the statue was intended only to show you, that by patience you will overcome all difficulties. Therefore, by no means let the notion of giants or magic dwell upon your minds. And you may farther observe, that there is a different style adapted to every sort of writing; and the various sounding epithets given to Barbarico are proper to express the raging cruelty of his wicked mind. But neither this high-sounding language, nor the supernatural contrivances in this story, do I so thoroughly approve, as to recommend them much to your reading; except, as I said before, great care is taken to prevent your being carried away, by these high-flown things, from that simplicity of taste and manners which it is my chief study to inculcate.'

Here Miss Jenny looked a little confounded; and, by her down-cast eye, showed a fear that she had incurred the disapprobation, if not the displeasure, of her governess: upon which Mrs. Teachum thus proceeded:

'I do not intend by this, my dear, to blame you for what you have done; but only to instruct you how to make the best use of even the most trifling things: and if you have any more stories of this kind, with an equal good moral, when you are not better employed, I shall not be against your reading them; always remembering the cautions I have this evening been giving you.'

Miss Jenny thanked her governess for her instructions, and kind indulgence to her, and promised to give her an exact account of their daily amusements; and, taking leave, retired to her rest.

TUESDAY. THE SECOND DAY.

That Miss Jenny's meeting with her companions in the morning, after school, she asked them how they liked the history of the giants? They all declared they thought it a very pretty diverting story. Miss Jenny replied, though she was glad they were pleased, yet she would have them look farther than the present amusement: 'for,' continued she, 'my mamma always taught me to understand what I read; otherwise, she said, it was to no manner of purpose to read ever so many books, which would only stuff my brain, without being any improvement to my mind.'

The misses all agreed, that certainly it was of no use to read, without understanding what they read; and began to talk of the story of the giants, to prove they could make just remarks on it.

Miss Sukey Jennett said, 'I am most pleased with that part of the story where the good Benefico cuts off the monster's head, and puts an end to his cruelty, especially as he was so sullen he would not confess his wickedness; because, you know, Miss Jenny, if he had had sense enough to have owned his error, and have followed the example of the good giant, he might have been happy.'

Miss Lucy Sly delivered the following opinion: 'My greatest joy was whilst Mignon was tying the magic fillet round the monster's neck, and conquering him.'

'Now I (said Miss Dolly Friendly) am most pleased with that part of the story, were Fidus and Amata meet the reward of their constancy and love, when they find each other after all their sufferings.'

Miss Polly Suckling said, with some eagerness, 'My greatest joy was in the description of Mignon; and to think that it should be in the power of that little creature to conquer such a great monster.'

Miss Patty Lockit, Miss Nanny Spruce, Miss Betty Ford, and Miss Henny Fret, advanced no new opinions; but agreed some to one, and some to another, of those that were already advanced. And as every one was eager to maintain her own opinion, an argument followed, the particulars of which I could never learn: only thus much I know, that it was concluded by Miss Lucy Sly, saying, with an air and tone of voice that implied more anger than had been heard since the reconciliation, that she was sure Miss Polly Suckling only liked that part about Mignon, because she was the least in the school; and Mignon being such a little creature, put her in mind of herself.

Miss Jenny Peace now began to be frighted, lest this contention should raise another quarrel; and therefore begged to be heard before they went any farther. They were not yet angry enough to refuse hearing what she had to say: and then Miss Jenny desired them to consider the moral of the story, and what use they might make of it, instead of contending which was the prettiest part: 'For otherwise,' continued she, 'I have lost my breath in reading to you; and you will be worse, rather than better, for what you have heard. Pray observe, that Benefico's happiness arose entirely from his goodness: he had less strength, and less riches, than the cruel monster; and yet, by the good use he made of what he possessed, you see how he turned all things to his advantage. But particularly remember, that the good little Mignon, in the moment that he was patiently submitting to his sufferings, found a method of relieving himself from them, and of overcoming a barbarous monster, who had so cruelly abused him.

'Our good governess last night not only instructed me in this moral I am now communicating to you, but likewise bid me warn you by no means to let the notion of giants or magic to dwell upon your minds; for by a giant is meant no more than a man of great power; and the magic fillet round the head of the statue was only intended to teach you, that by the assistance of patience you may overcome all difficulties.

'In order therefore to make what you read of any use to you, you must not only think of it thus in general, but make the application to yourselves. For when (as now) instead of improving yourselves by reading, you make what you read a subject to quarrel about, what is this less than being like the monster Barbarico, who turned his very riches to a curse? I am sure it is not following the example of Benefico, who made everything a blessing to him. Remember, if you pinch and abuse a dog or cat, because it is in your power, you are like the cruel Monster, when he abused the little Mignon, and said,

I am a giant, and I can eat thee;   *Thou art a dwarf, and thou canst not eat me.*

'In short, if you will reap any benefit from this story towards rendering you happy, whenever you have any power, you must follow the example of the giant Benefico, and do good with it: and when you are under any sufferings, like Mignon, you must patiently endure them till you can find a remedy: then, in one case, like Benefico, you will enjoy what you possess; and, in the other, you will in time, like Mignon, overcome your sufferings: for the natural consequence of indulging cruelty and revenge in the mind, even where there is the highest power to gratify it, is misery.'

Here Miss Sukey Jennet interrupted Miss Jenny, saying, that she herself had experienced the truth of that observation in the former part of her life: for she never had known either peace or pleasure, till she had conquered in her mind the desire of hurting and being revenged on those who she thought did not by their behaviour show the same regard for her, that her own good opinion of herself made her think she deserved. Miss Jenny then asked her, if she was willing to lead the way to the rest of her companions, by telling her past life? She answered, she would do it with all her heart; and, by having so many and great faults to confess, she hoped she should, by her true confessions, set them an example of honesty and ingenuity.

THE DESCRIPTION OF MISS SUKEY JENNETT.

Miss Sukey Jennett, who was next in years to Miss Jenny Peace, was not quite twelve years old; but so very tall of her age, that she was within a trifle as tall as Miss Jenny Peace; and, by growing so fast, was much thinner: and though she was not really so well made, yet, from an assured air in her manner of carrying herself, she was called much the genteelest girl. There was, on first view, a great resemblance in their persons. Her face was very handsome, and her complexion extremely good; but a little more inclined to pale than Miss Jenny's. Her eyes were a degree darker, and had a life and fire in them which was very beautiful: but yet her impatience on the least contradiction often brought a fierceness into her eyes, and gave such a discomposure to her whole countenance, as immediately took off your admiration. But her eyes had now, since her hearty reconciliation with her companions, lost a great part of their fierceness; and with great mildness, and an obliging manner, she told her story as follows:

THE LIFE OF MISS SUKEY JENNETT.

'My mamma died when I was so young that I cannot remember her; and my papa marrying again within half a year after her death, I was chiefly left to the care of an old servant, that had lived many years in the family. I was a great favourite of hers, and in everything had my own way. When I was but four years old, if ever anything crossed me, I was taught to beat it, and be revenged of it, even though it could not feel. If I fell down and hurt myself, the very ground was to be beat for hurting the sweet child: so that, instead of fearing to fall, I did not dislike it; for I was pleased to find, that I was of such consequence, that everything was to take care that I came by no harm.

'I had a little playfellow, in a child of one of my papa's servants, who was to be entirely under my command. This girl I used to abuse and beat, whenever I was out of humour; and when I had abused her, if she dared to grumble, or make the least complaint, I thought it the greatest impudence in the world; and, instead of mending my behaviour to her, I grew very angry that she should dare to dispute my power: for my governess always told her, that she was but a servant's girl, and I was a gentleman's daughter; and that therefore she ought to give way to me; for that I did her great honour in playing with her. Thus I thought the distance between us was so great, that I never considered that she could feel: but whilst I myself suffered nothing, I fancied everything was very right; and it never once came into my head, that I could be in the wrong.

'This life I led till I came to school, when I was eleven years old. Here I had nobody in my power; for all my schoolfellows thought themselves my equals: so that I could only quarrel, fight, and contend for everything: but being liable to be punished, when I was trying to be revenged on any of my enemies, as I thought them, I never had a moment's ease or pleasure, till Miss Jenny was so good to take the pains to convince me of my folly, and made me be reconciled to you, my dear companions.'

Here Miss Sukey ceased; and Miss Jenny smiled with pleasure, at the thoughts that she had been the cause of her happiness.

Mrs. Teachum being now come into the arbour, to see in what manner her little scholars passed their time, they all rose up and do her reverence. Miss Jenny gave her an account how they had been employed; and she was much pleased with their innocent and useful entertainment; but especially with the method they had found out of relating their past lives. She took little Polly Suckling by the hand, and bidding the rest follow, it being now dinner time, she walked towards the house, attended by the whole company.

Mrs. Teachum had a great inclination to hear the history of the lives of all her little scholars: but she thought, that being present at those relations might be a balk to the narration, as perhaps they might be ashamed freely to confess their past faults before her; and therefore, that she might not be any bar in this case to the freedom of their speech, and yet might be acquainted with their stories (though this was not merely a vain curiosity, but a desire by this means to know their different dispositions), she called Miss Jenny Peace to her parlour after dinner, and told her, she would have her get the lives of her companions in writing, and bring them to her; and Miss Jenny readily promised to obey her commands.

In the evening our little company again met in their charming arbour; where they were no sooner seated, with that calmness and content which now always attended them, than the cries and sobs of a child, at a little distance from their garden, disturbed their tranquility.

Miss Jenny, ever ready to relieve the distressed, ran immediately to the place whence the sound seemed to come, and was followed by all her companions: when, at a small distance from Mrs. Teachum's garden-wall, over which from the terrace our young company looked, they saw, under a large spreading tree, part of the branches of which shaded a seat at the end of that terrace, a middle aged woman beating a little girl, who looked to be about eight years old, so severely, that it was no wonder her cries had reached their arbour.

Miss Jenny could not forbear calling out to the woman, and begging her to forbear: and little Polly Suckling cried as much as the girl, and desired she might not be beat any more. The woman, in respect to them, let the child go; but said, 'Indeed, young ladies, you don't know what a naughty girl she is: for though you now see me correct her in this manner, yet am I in all respects very kind to her, and never strike her but for lying. I have tried all means, good and bad, to break her of this vile fault; but hitherto all I have done has been in vain: nor can I ever get one word of truth out of her mouth. But I am resolved to break her of this horrid custom, or I cannot live with her: for though I am but poor, yet I will breed up my child to be honest, both in word and deed.'

Miss Jenny could not but approve of what the poor woman said. However, they all joined in begging forgiveness for the girl this time, provided she promised amendment for the future: and then our little society returned to their arbour.

Miss Jenny could not help expressing her great detestation of all lying whatsoever; when Miss Dolly Friendly, colouring, confessed she had often been guilty of this fault, though she never scarcely did it but for her friend.

Here Miss Jenny, interrupting her, said, that even that was no sort of excuse for lying; besides that the habit of it on any occasion, even with the appearance of a good intention, would but too likely lead to the use of it on many others: and as she did not doubt, by Miss Dolly's blushing, that she was now very sensible of the truth of what she had just been saying, she hoped she would take this opportunity of obliging them with the history of her past life: which request she made no hesitation to grant, saying, the shame of her past faults should by o means induce her to conceal them.

THE DESCRIPTION OF MISS DOLLY FRIENDLY.

Miss Dolly Friendly was just turned of eleven years of age. Her person was neither plain nor handsome: and though she had not what is properly called one fine feature in her face, yet the disposition of them were so suitable to each other, that her countenance was rather agreeable than otherwise. She had generally something very quiet, or rather indolent, in her look, except when she was moved by anger; which seldom happened, but in defense of some favourite or friend; and she had then a fierceness and eagerness which altered her whole countenance: for she could not bear the least reflection or insult on those she loved. This disposition made her always eager to comply with her friends' requests; and she immediately began, as follows:

THE LIFE OF MISS DOLLY FRIENDLY.

'I was bred up, till I was nine years of age, with a sister, who was one year younger than myself. The chief care of our parents was to make us love each other; and, as I was naturally inclined to have very strong affections, I became so fond of my sister Molly, which was her name, that all my delight was to please her; and this I carried to such a height, that I scrupled no lies to excuse her faults: and whatever she did, I justified, and thought right, only because she did it.

'I was ready to fight her quarrels, whether right or wrong; and hated everybody that offended her. My parents winked at whatever I did in defence of my sister; and I had no notion that any thing done for her could be unreasonable. In short, I made it my study to oblige and please her, till I found at last it was out of my power; for she grew so very humoursome, that she could not find out what she had most mind to have; and I found her always miserable; for she would cry only because she did not know her own mind.

'She never minded what faults she committed, because she knew I would excuse her; and she was forgiven in consideration of our friendship, which gave our parents great pleasure.

'My poor little sister grew very sickly, and she died just before I came to school: but the same disposition still continued; and it was my friend's outcries of being hurt, that drew me into that odious quarrel, that we have all now repented.'

Here Miss Dolly Friendly ceased; and Miss Jenny said, she hoped Miss Dolly would remember, for the rest of her life, what HER good mamma had always taught her; namely, that it was not the office of friendship, to justify or excuse our friend when in the wrong; for that was the way to prevent their ever being in the right: that it was rather hatred, or contempt, than love, when the fear of another's anger made us forego their good, for the sake of our own present pleasure; and that the friends who expected such flattery were not worth keeping.

The bell again summoned our little company to supper: but, before they went in, Miss Dolly Friendly said, if Miss Jenny approved of it, she would the next morning read them a story given her by an uncle of hers, that, she said, she was sure would please her, as its subject was friendship. Miss Jenny replied, that she was certain it would be a great pleasure to them all, to hear any story Miss Dolly thought proper to read them.

WEDNESDAY. THE THIRD DAY.

As soon as school was over in the morning, our little company were impatient to go into the arbour, to hear Miss Dolly's story: but Mrs. Teachum told them they must be otherwise employed; for their writing-master, who lived some miles off; and who was expected in the afternoon, was just then come in, and begged that they would give him their attendance, though out of school-time; because he was obliged to be at home again before the afternoon, to meet a person who would confer some favour on him, and would be highly disobliged should he not keep his appointment: 'And I know (said Mrs. Teachum) my little dears, you would rather lose your own amusement, than let any one suffer a real inconvenience on your accounts.' They all readily complied, and cheerfully set to their writing; and in the afternoon Mrs. Teachum permitted them to leave off work an hour sooner than usual, as a reward for their readiness to lose their amusement in the morning: and being met in their arbour, Miss Dolly read as follows:

THE STORY OF CAELIA AND CHLOE.

Caelia and Chloe were both left orphans, at the tender age of six years. Amanda their aunt, who was very rich, and a maiden, took them directly under her care, and bred them up as her own children. Caelia's mother was Amanda's sister; and Chloe's father was her brother; so that she was equally related to both.

They were left entirely unprovided for; were both born on the same day; and both lost their mothers on the day of their birth: their fathers were soldiers of fortune; and both killed in one day, in the fame engagement. But their fortunes were not more similar than their persons and dispositions. They were both extremely handsome; and in their Childhood were so remarkable for liveliness of parts, and sweetness of temper, that they were the admiration of the whole country where they lived.

Their aunt loved them with a sincere and equal affection, and took the greatest pleasure imaginable in their education, and particularly to encourage that love and friendship which she with pleasure perceived between them. Amanda being (as was said) very rich, and having no other relations, it was supposed that these her nieces would be very great fortunes; and as soon as they became women, they were addressed by all the men of fortune and no fortune round the neighbourhood. But as the love of admiration, and a desire of a large train of admirers, had no place in their minds, they soon dismissed, in the most civil and obliging manner, one after another, all these lovers.

The refusing such numbers of men, and some such as by the world were called good offers, soon got them the name of jilts; and by that means they were freed from any farther importunity, and for some years enjoyed that peace and quiet they had long wished. Their aunt, from being their mother and their guardian, was now become their friend. For, as she endeavoured not in the least to force their inclinations, they never kept anything concealed from her; and every action of their lives was still guided by her advice and approbation.

They lived on in this way, perfectly happy in their own little community, till they were about two-and-twenty years old when there happened to be a regiment quartered in the neighbouring town, to which their house was nearly situated; and the lieutenant-colonel, a man about four-and-thirty years old, hearing their names, had a great desire to see them. For when he was a boy of sixteen, he was put into the Army under the care of Chloe's father, who treated him with the greatest tenderness; and (in that fatal engagement in which he lost his life) received his death's wound by endeavouring to save him from being taken by the enemy. And gratitude to the memory of so good a friend was as great an inducement to make him desire to see his daughter, as the report he had heard both of hers and her cousin's great beauty.

Sempronius (for so this Colonel was called) was a very sensible, well-bred, agreeable man; and from the circumstances of his former acquaintance, and his present proper and polite behaviour, he soon became very intimate in the family. The old lady was particularly pleased with him; and secretly wished, that before she died she might be so happy as to see one of her nieces married to Sempronius. She could not from his behaviour see the least particular liking to either, though he showed an equal and very great esteem and regard for both.

He in reality liked them both extremely; and the reason of making no declaration of love was, his being so undetermined in any preference that was due to either. He saw plainly that he was very agreeable to both; and with pleasure he observed, that they made use of none of those arts which women generally do to get away a disputed lover: and this sincere friendship which subsisted between them raised in him the highest degree of love and admiration. However he at last determined to make the following trial:

He went first to Chloe, and (finding her alone) told her, that he had the greatest liking in the world to her cousin; and had really a mind to propose himself to her: but as he saw a very great friendship between them, he was willing to ask her advice in the matter; and conjured her to tell him sincerely, whether there was anything in Caelia's temper (not discoverable by him) which as a wife would make him unhappy? He told her, that, if she knew any such thing, it would be no treachery, but rather kind in her to declare it, as it would prevent her friend's being unhappy; which must be the consequence, in marriage, of her making him so.

Chloe could not help seeing very plainly, that if Caelia was removed she stood the very next in Sempronius's favour. Her lover was present—her friend was absent—and the temptation was too strong and agreeable to be resisted. She then answered, that since he insisted upon the truth, and had convinced her that it was in reality acting justly and kindly by her friend, she must confess, that Caelia was possessed (though in a very small degree) of what she had often heard him declare most against of anything in the world; and that was, an artfulness of temper, and some few sparks of envy.

Chloe's confused manner of speaking, and frequent hesitation, as unwilling to pronounce her friend's condemnation (which, as being unused to falsehood, was really unaffected) he imputed to tenderness and concern for Caelia; but he did not in the least doubt, but on his application to her he should soon be convinced of the truth of what Chloe had said.

He then went directly to the arbour at the end of the garden, and there to his wish he found Caelia quite alone; and he addressed her exactly in the same manner concerning her cousin, as he had before spoke to Chloe concerning her. Caelia suddenly blushed (from motives I leave those to find out who can put themselves in her circumstances) and then fetched a soft sigh, from the thought that she was hearing a man she loved declare a passion of which she was not the object. But after some little pause, she told him, that if Chloe had any faults, they were to her yet undiscovered, and she really and sincerely believed her cousin would make him extremely happy. Sempronius then said, that of all other things, TREACHERY and ENVY were what he had the greatest dislike to: and he asked her, if she did not think her cousin was a little tainted with these?—Here Caelia could not help interrupting, and assuring him, that she believed her totally free from both. And, from his casting on her friend an aspersion which her very soul abhorred, forgetting all rivalship, she could not refrain from growing quite lavish in her praise. 'Suppose then (said Sempronius) I was to say the same to your cousin concerning my intentions towards you as I have to you concerning her, do you think she would say as many fine things in your praise as you have done in hers?'

Caelia answered, that she verily believed her cousin would say as much for her as she really deserved; but whether that would be equal to what with justice she could say of Chloe, her modesty left her in some doubt of.

Sempronius had too much penetration not to see the real and true difference in the behaviour of these two women, and could not help crying out, 'O Caelia! your honest truth and goodness in every word and look are too visible to leave me one doubt of their reality. But, could you believe it? this friend of yours is false. I have already put her to the trial, by declaring to her my sincere and unalterable passion for you. When, on my insisting, as I did to you, upon her speaking the truth, she accused you of what nothing should now convince me you are guilty of. I own, that hitherto my regard, esteem, and love, have been equal to both; but now I offer to the sincere, artless, and charming Caelia, my whole heart, love, and affection, and the service of every minute of my future life; and from this moment I banish from my mind the false and ungrateful Chloe.'

Caelia's friendship for Chloe was so deeply rooted in her breast, that even a declaration of love from Sempronius could not blot it one moment from her heart; and on his speaking the words 'false Chloe,' she burst into tears, and said, 'Is it possible that Chloe should act such a part towards her Caelia! You must forgive her, Sempronius: it was her violent passion for you, and fear of losing you, which made her do what hitherto her nature has ever appeared averse to.'

Sempronius answered, 'that he could not enough admire her goodness to her friend Chloe; but such proofs of passion, he said, were to him at the same time proofs of its being such a passion as he had no regard for; since it was impossible for any one to gain or increase his love by an action which at the same time lessened his esteem.' This was so exactly Caelia's own way of thinking, that she could not but assent to what he said.

But just as they were coming out of the arbour, Chloe, unseen by them, passed by; and from seeing him kiss her hand, and the complacency of Caelia's look, it was easy for her to guess what had been the result of their private conference. She could not however help indulging her curiosity, so far as to walk on the other side of a thick yew hedge, to listen to their discourse; and as they walked on, she heard Sempronius entreat Caelia to be cheerful, and think no more of her treacherous friend, whose wickedness he doubted not would sufficiently punish itself. She then heard Caelia say, 'I cannot bear, Sempronius, to hear you speak so hardly of my Chloe. Say that you forgive her, and I will indeed be cheerful.'

Nothing upon earth can be conceived so wretched as poor Chloe, for on the first moment that she suffered herself to reflect on what she had done, she thoroughly repented, and heartily detested herself for such baseness. She went directly into the garden in hopes of meeting Sempronius, to have thrown herself at his feet, confessed her treachery, and to have begged him never to have mentioned it to Caelia; but now she was conscious her repentance would come too late; and he would despise her, if possible still more, for such a recantation, after her knowledge of what had passed between him and Caelia.

She could indeed have gone to him, and not have owned what she had seen or heard; but now her abhorrence of even the appearance of treachery or cunning was so great, that she could not bear to add the smallest grain of falsehood or deceit to the weight of her guilt, which was already almost insupportable: and should she tell him of her repentance, with a confession of her knowledge of his engagement with Caelia, it would (as has been before observed) appear both servile and insincere.

Nothing could now appear so altered as the whole face of this once happy family. Sempronius as much as possible shunned the sight of Chloe; for as she was the cause of all the confusion amongst them, he had almost an aversion to her. Though he was not of an implacable temper, yet, as the injury was intended to one he sincerely loved, he found it much harder to forgive it, than if it had even succeeded against himself; and as he still looked upon Chloe as the cause of melancholy in his dear Caelia, he could hardly have any patience with her.

No words can describe the various passions which were expressed in the sad countenance of Chloe, when first she met her friend. They were both afraid of speaking. Shame, and the fear of being (and with too good reason) suspected of insincerity, withheld Chloe; and an unwillingness to accuse or hurt her friend withheld the gentle Caelia. She sometimes indeed thought she saw repentance in Chloe's face, and wished for nothing more than to seal her pardon. But till it was asked, she was in doubt (from what had passed) whether such pardon and proffered reconciliation might not be rejected. She knew that her friend's passions were naturally stronger than hers; and she therefore trembled at the consequences of coming to an explanation.

But there was hardly a greater sufferer in this scene of confusion than the poor old Lady Amanda. She saw a sort of horror and wildness in the face of Chloe; and in Caelia's a settled melancholy, and such an unusual reserve in both towards each other, as well as to herself, as quite astonished her.

Sempronius came indeed to the house as often as usual; but in his countenance she could perceive a sort of anger and concern which perfectly frightened her. But as they did not speak to her, she could not bring herself to ask the cause of this woeful change, for fear of hearing something too bad to bear.

Caelia had absolutely refused granting to Sempronius leave to ask her aunt's consent, till she should come to some explanation with Chloe, which seemed every day farther off than ever.

The great perturbation of Chloe's mind threw her into a disorder not many degrees short of madness; and at last she was seized with a violent fever so as to keep her bed. She said she could not bear to look on Amanda; but begged Caelia to be with her as much as possible; which she did, in hopes of bringing herself to ease her mind, by speaking to her of what had given them all this torment.

Caelia watched with her night and day for three days, when the physician who attended her pronounced that there was no hope of her life. Caelia could not any longer bear to stay in the room, and went downstairs, expecting every moment to hear she was expired.

Chloe soon perceived by Caelia's abrupt leaving the room, and the looks of those who were left in it, that her fate was pronounced; which, instead of sinking her spirits, and making her dejected, gave a tranquillity to her mind; for she thought within herself, 'I shall now make my dear cousin happy, by removing out of her way an object that must embitter all her joy; and now likewise, as she is convinced I am on my death-bed, she will once more believe me capable of speaking truth; and will, in the manner I could wish, receive my sincere repentance.' Then sending for Caelia up to her bedside, she in a weak voice, with hardly strength for utterance, spoke in this manner: 'My dear Caelia, though you know me to be a worthless base wretch, yet do not think so hardly of me, as to imagine I would deceive you with my last breath. Believe me then when I tell you, that I sincerely repent of my treachery towards you; and as sincerely rejoice that it has in reality been the cause of your happiness with Sempronius. Tell him this; and then, perhaps, he will not hate my memory.' Here she fainted away, and they forced Caelia out of the room, thinking her breath was for ever flown. But in some time she came again to herself, and cried out, 'What! would not my dear Caelia say that she forgave me? Methinks I would not die, till I had obtained her pardon. She is too good to refuse her friend this last request.' Her attendants then told her, that seeing her faint away, they had forced Caelia out of the room; and they begged her to try to compose herself, for they were sure that seeing her friend again, at this time, would only disturb her mind, and do her an injury.

Chloe, from the vent she had given her grief in speaking to Caelia, found herself something more easy and composed; and desiring the room to be made perfectly quiet, she fell into a gentle sleep, which lasted two hours; and when she awaked she found herself so much better, that those about her were convinced, from her composed manner of speaking, that she was now able to bear another interview.

They again called for Caelia, and told her of her cousin's amendment. She flew with all speed to her chamber; and the moment she entered, Chloe cried out, 'Can you forgive me, Caelia?' 'Yes, with the greatest joy and sincerity imaginable, my dearest Chloe,' answered Caelia, 'and never let it be again mentioned or remembered.'

The sudden recovery of Chloe was almost incredible; for in less than a week she was able to quit both her bed and room, and go into her aunt's chamber. The good old lady shed tears of joy, to see such a return of Chloe's health, and of cheerfulness in the family; and was perfectly contented, now she saw their melancholy removed, not to inquire into the late cause of it, for fear of renewing their trouble even one moment by the remembrance of it.

Sempronius, in the meantime, upon some affairs of his duty in the army, had been called away, and was absent the whole time of Chloe's illness, and was not yet returned. Caelia spent almost her whole time with Chloe; but three weeks passed on, and they were often alone; yet they had never once mentioned the name of Sempronius, which laid Caelia still under the greatest difficulty how to act, so as to avoid giving her friend any uneasiness, and yet not disoblige Sempronius; for she had promised him at his departure, that she would give him leave to ask her aunt's consent immediately upon his return. But the very day he was expected, she was made quite easy by what passed between her and her friend.

Chloe, in this time, by proper reflections, and a due sense of Caelia's great goodness and affection to her, had so entirely got the better of herself in this affair, that she found she could now, without any uneasiness, see them married; and calling Caelia to her, she said with a smile, 'I have, my dear friend, been so long accustomed to read in that intelligible index, your countenance, all your most inmost thoughts, that I have not been unobserving of those kind fears you have had on my account; and the reason I have so long delayed speaking was, my resolution, if possible, never again to deceive you. I can with pleasure now assure you, that nothing can give me so much joy as to see your wedding with Sempronius. I make no doubt, but if you ask it, you will have my aunt's consent; and, if any intercession should be wanting towards obtaining it, I will (if you can trust me) use all my influence in your behalf. Be assured, my dear Caelia, I have now no farther regard left for Sempronius, than as your husband; and that regard will increase in proportion as he is the cause of your happiness.'

They were interrupted in their discourse by news being brought of the arrival of Sempronius, and Chloe received him with that ease and cheerfulness as convinced Caelia her professions were unfeigned.

Caelia related to Sempronius all that had passed between her and Chloe; and by her continued cheerfulness of behaviour, the peace and tranquillity of the family was perfectly restored, and their joy greatly increased by Amanda's ready consent to the marriage of Sempronius and Caelia, having first settled all her fortune to be divided at her death equally between her nieces; and in her lifetime there was no occasion of settlements, or deeds of gift, for they lived all together, and separate property was not so much as mentioned or thought on in this family of harmony and peace.

Here Miss Dolly ceased reading; and all her hearers sat some little time silent, and then expressed their great joy that Caelia and Chloe were at last happy; for none of them had been able to refrain from tears whilst they were otherwise. On which Miss Jenny Peace begged them to observe from this story, the miserable effects that attend deceit and treachery: 'For,' continued she, 'you see you could not refrain from tears, only by imagining what Chloe must feel after her wickedness (by which indeed she lost the very happiness she intended treacherously to gain); nor could she enjoy one moment's peace, till by confessing her fault, and heartily repenting of it, her mind was restored to its former calm and tranquility.' Miss Dolly thanked Miss Jenny for her remarks; but Miss Lucy Sly was most sensibly touched with this story, as cunning had formerly entirely possessed HER mind; and said, that if her companions were not weary at present of their arbour, she would now recount to them the history of her life, as this story was a proper introduction to it.

THE DESCRIPTION OF MISS LUCY SLY.

Miss Lucy Sly was of the same age as Miss Dolly Friendly, but shorter, at least, by half the head. She was generally called a pretty girl, from having a pair of exceeding fine black eyes, only with the allay of something cunning in their look. She had a high forehead, and very good curling black hair. She had a sharp high nose, and a very small mouth. Her complexion was but indifferent, and the lower part of her face ill-turned, for her chin was too long for due proportion.

THE LIFE OF MISS LUCY SLY.

From the time I was two years old, (said Miss Lucy) my mamma was so sickly, that she was unable to take any great care of me herself, and I was left to the care of a governess, who made it her study to bring me to do what she had a mind to have done, without troubling her head what induced me so to do. And whenever I did anything wrong, she used to say it was the foot-boy, and not miss, that was naughty. Nay, she would say, it was the dog, or the cat, or anything she could lay the blame upon, sooner than own it was me. I thought this pure, that I was never in fault; and soon got into a way of telling any lies, and of laying my own faults on others, since I found I should be believed. I remember once, when I had broken a fine china-cup, that I artfully got out of the scrape, and hid the broken cup in the foot-boy's room. He was whipped for breaking it; and the next day whilst I was at play about the room, I heard my governess say to a friend who was with her, "Yesterday Miss Lucy broke a china-cup; but the artful little hussy went and hid it in the foot-boy's room, and the poor boy was whipped for it. I don't believe there was ever a girl of her age that had half her cunning and contrivance." I knew by her tone of voice, and her manner of speaking, that she did not blame me in her heart, but rather commended my ingenuity. And I thought myself so wise, that I could thus get off the blame from myself, that I every day improved in new inventions to save myself, and have others punished in my place.

'This life of endeavouring to deceive I led till I came to school. But here I found that I could not so well carry on my little schemes; for I was found out and punished for my own faults; and this created in me a hatred to my companions. For whatever Miss I had a mind to serve as I used to serve our foot-boy, in laying the blame falsely upon her, if she could justify herself, and prove me in the wrong, I was very angry with her, for daring to contradict me, and not submitting as quietly to be punished wrongfully, as the foot-boy was forced to do.

'This is all I know of my life hitherto.'

Thus ended Miss Lucy Sly: and Miss Jenny Peace commended Miss Lucy for her free confession of her faults, and said, 'She doubted not but she would find the advantage of amending, and endeavouring to change a disposition so very pernicious to her own peace and quiet, as well as to that of all her friends;' but they now obeyed the summons of the supper-bell, and soon after retired to rest.

THURSDAY. THE FOURTH DAY.

Our little company, as soon as the morning school-hours were over, hastened to their arbour, and were attentive to what Miss Jenny Peace should propose to them for their amusement till dinner-time; when Miss Jenny, looking round upon them, said, 'that she had not at present any story to read; but that she hoped, from Miss Dolly Friendly's example yesterday, some of the rest might endeavour sometimes to furnish out the entertainment of the day.' Upon which Miss Sukey Jennett said, 'that though she could not promise them such an agreeable story as Miss Dolly's; yet she would read them a letter she had received the evening before from her Cousin Peggy Smith, who lived at York; in which there was a story that she thought very strange and remarkable. They were all very desirous of it, when Miss Sukey read as follows:

'Dear cousin,—I promised, you know, to write to you when I had anything to tell you; and as I think the following story very extraordinary, I was willing to keep my word.

'Some time ago there came to settle in this city, a lady, whose name was Dison. We all visited her: but she had so deep a melancholy, arising, as it appeared, from a settled state of ill health, that nothing we could do could afford her the least relief, or make her cheerful. In this condition she languished amongst us five years, still continuing to grow worse and worse.

'We all grieved at her fate. Her flesh was withered away; her appetite decayed by degrees, till all food became nauseous to her sight; her strength failed her; her feet could not support her tottering body, lean and worn away as it was; and we hourly expected her death. When, at last, she one day called her most intimate friends to her bedside, and, as well as she could, spoke to the following purpose: "I know you all pity me; but, alas! I am not so much the object of your pity, as your contempt; for all my misery is of my own seeking, and owing to the wickedness of my own mind. I had two sisters, with whom I was bred up; and I have all my lifetime been unhappy, for no other cause but for their success in the world. When we were young, I could neither eat nor sleep in peace, when they had either praise or pleasure. When we grew up to be women, they were both soon married much to their advantage and satisfaction. This galled me to the heart; and, though I had several good offers, yet as I did not think them in all respects equal to my sisters, I would not accept them; and yet was inwardly vexed to refuse them, for fear I would get no better. I generally deliberated so long that I lost my lovers, and then I pined for that loss. I never wanted for anything; and was in a situation in which I might have been happy, if I pleased. My sisters loved me very well, for I concealed as much as possible from them my odious envy; and yet never did any poor wretch lead so miserable a life as I have done; for every blessing they enjoyed was as so many daggers to my heart. 'Tis this envy that has caused all my ill health, has preyed upon my very vitals, and will now bring me to my Grave."

'In a few days after this confession she died; and her words and death made such a strong impression on my mind, that I could not help sending you this relation; and begging you, my dear Sukey, to remember how careful we ought to be to curb in our minds the very first risings of a passion so detestable, and so fatal, as this proved to poor Mrs. Dison. I know I have no particular reason for giving you this caution; for I never saw anything in you, but what deserved the love and esteem of

'Your very affectionate cousin,

'M. SMITH.'

As soon as Miss Sukey had finished her letter, Miss Patty Lockit rose up, and, flying to Miss Jenny Peace, embraced her, and said, 'What thanks can I give you, my dear friend, for having put me into a way of examining my heart, and reflecting on my own actions; by which you have saved me, perhaps, from a life as miserable as that of the poor woman in Miss Sukey's letter!' Miss Jenny did not thoroughly understand her meaning; but imagining it might be something relating to her past life, desired her to explain herself; which she said she would do, telling now, in her turn, all that had hitherto happened to her.

THE DESCRIPTION OF MISS PATTY LOCKIT.

Miss Patty Lockit was but ten years old; tall, inclined to fat. Her neck was short; and she was not in the least genteel. Her face was very handsome; for all her features were extremely good. She had large blue eyes; was exceeding fair; and had a great bloom on her cheeks. Her hair was the very first degree of light brown; was bright and shining; and hung in ringlets half way down her back. Her mouth was rather too large; but she had such fine teeth, and looked so agreeably when she smiled, that you was not sensible of any fault in it.

This was the person of Miss Patty Lockit, who was slow to relate her past life; which she did, in the following manner:

THE LIFE OF MISS PATTY LOCKIT.

I lived, till I was six years old, in a very large family; for I had four sisters, all older than myself, and three brothers. We played together, and passed our time much in the common way: sometimes we quarrelled, and sometimes agreed, just as accident would have it. Our parents had no partiality to any of us; so we had no cause to envy one another on that account; and we lived tolerably well together.

'When I was six years old, my grandmother by my father's side (and who was also my godmother) offering to take me to live with her, and promising to look upon me as her own child, and entirely to provide for me, my father and mother, as they had a large family, very readily accepted her offer, and sent me directly to her house.

'About half a year before this, she had taken another goddaughter, the only child of my Aunt Bradly, who was lately dead, and whose husband was gone to the West Indies. My cousin, Molly Bradly, was four years older than I; and her mother had taken such pains in her education, that the understood more than most girls of her age; and had so much liveliness, good humour, and ingenuity, that everybody was fond of her; and wherever we went together, all the notice was taken of my cousin, and I was very little regarded.

'Though I had all my life before lived in a family where every one in it was older, and knew more than myself, yet I was very easy; for we were generally together in the nursery; and nobody took much notice of us, whether we knew anything, or whether we did not. But now, as I lived in the house with only one companion, who was so much more admired than myself, the comparison began to vex me, and I found a strong hatred and aversion for my cousin arising in my mind; and yet, I verily believe I should have got the better of it, and been willing to have learnt of my cousin, and should have loved her for teaching me, if any one had told me it was right; and if it had not been that Betty, the maid who took care of us, used to be for ever teasing me about the preference that was shown to my cousin, and the neglect I always met with. She used to tell me, that she wondered how I could bear to see Miss Molly so caressed; and that it was want of spirit not to think myself as good as she was; and, if she was in my place, she would not submit to be taught by a child; for my Cousin Molly frequently offered to instruct me in anything she knew; but I used to say (as Betty had taught me) that I would not learn of her; for she was but a child, though she was a little older; and that I was not put under her care, but that of my grandmamma. But she, poor woman, was so old and unhealthy, that she never troubled her head much about us, but only to take care that we wanted for nothing. I lived in this manner three years, fretting and vexing myself that I did not know so much, nor was not so much liked, as my Cousin Molly, and yet resolving not to learn anything she could teach me; when my grandmamma was advised to send me to school; but, as soon as I came here, the case was much worse; for, instead of one person to envy, I found many; for all my schoolfellows had learned more than I; and, instead of endeavouring to get knowledge, I began to hate all those who knew more than myself; and this, I am now convinced, was owing to that odious envy, which, if not cured, would always have made me as miserable as Mrs. Dison was and which constantly tormented me, till we came to live in that general peace and good-humour we have lately enjoyed: and as I hope this wicked spirit was not natural to me, but only blown up by that vile Betty's instigations, I don't doubt but I shall now grow very happy, and learn something every day, and be pleased with being instructed, and that I shall always love those who are so good as to instruct me.'

Here Miss Patty Lockit ceased; and the dinner-bell called them from their arbour.

Mrs. Teachum, as soon as they had dined, told them, that she thought it proper they would use some bodily exercise, that they might not, by sitting constantly still, impair their health. Not but that she was greatly pleased with their innocent and instructive manner of employing their leisure hours; but this wise woman knew that the faculties of the mind grow languid and useless, when the health of the body is lost.

As soon as they understood their governess's pleasure, they readily resolved to obey her commands, and desired that, after school, they might take a walk as far as the dairy house, to eat some curds and cream. Mrs. Teachum not only granted their request, but said she would dispense with their school-attendance that afternoon, in order to give them more time for their walk, which was between two and three miles; and she likewise added, that she herself would go with them. They all flew like lightning to get their hats, and to equip themselves for their walk; and, with cheerful countenances, attended Mrs. Teachum in the schoolroom. This good gentlewoman, so far from laying them under a restraint by her presence, encouraged them to run in the fields, and to gather flowers; which they did, each miss trying to get the best to present to her governess. In this agreeable manner, with laughing, talking, and singing, they arrived at the dairy-house, before they imagined they had walked a mile.

There lived at this dairy-house an old woman, near seventy years of age. She had a fresh colour in her face; but was troubled with the palsy, that made her head shake a little. She was bent forward with age, and her hair was quite grey: but she retained much good-humour, and received this little party with hearty welcome.

Our little gentry flocked about this good woman, asking her a thousand questions. Miss Polly Suckling asked her, 'Why she shook her head so?' and Miss Patty Lockit said, 'She hoped her hair would never be of such a colour.'

Miss Jenny Peace was afraid they would say something that would offend the old woman, and advised them to turn their discourse. 'Oh! let the dear rogues alone,' says the old woman; 'I like their prattle;' and, taking Miss Polly by the hand, said, 'Come, my dear, we will go into the dairy, and skim the milk pans.' At which words they all run into the dairy, and some of them dipped their fingers in the cream; which when Mrs. Nelly perceived (who was the eldest daughter of the old woman, and who managed all the affairs) she desired they would walk out of the dairy, and she would bring them what was fit for them: upon which Miss Dolly Friendly said, 'she had rather be as old and good-natured as the mother, than as young and ill-natured as the daughter.'

The old woman desired her company to sit down at a long table, which she soon supplied with plenty of cream, strawberries, brown bread, and sugar. Mrs. Teachum took her place at the upper end, and the rest sat down in their usual order, and eat plentifully of these good things. After which, Mrs. Teachum told them they might walk out and see the garden and orchard, and by that time it would be proper to return home.

The good old woman showed them the way into the garden; and gathered the finest roses and pinks she could pick, and gave them to Miss Polly, to whom she had taken a great Fancy.

At their taking leave, Mrs. Teachum rewarded the good old woman for her trouble; who, on her part, expressed much pleasure in feeing so many well-behaved young ladies; and said, she hoped they would come often.

These little friends had not walked far in their way home, before they met a miserable ragged fellow, who begged their charity. Our young folks immediately gathered together about this poor creature, and were hearkening very earnestly to his story, which he set forth in a terrible manner, of having been burnt out of his house, and, from one distress to another, reduced to that miserable state they saw him in, when Mrs. Teachum came up to them. She was not a little pleased to see all the misses' hands in their pockets, pulling out half-pence, and some sixpences. She told them, she approved of their readiness to assist the poor fellow, as he appeared to them; but oftentimes those fellows made up dismal stories without much foundation, and because they were lazy, and would not work. Miss Dolly said, indeed she believed the poor man spoke truth; for he looked honest; and, besides, he seemed almost starved.

Mrs. Teachum told them it would be late before they could get home; so, after each of them had given what they thought proper, they pursued their walk, prattling all the way.

They got home about nine o'clock; and, as they did not choose any supper, the bell rang for prayers; after which our young travellers retired to their rest, where we doubt not but they had a good repose.

FRIDAY. THE FIFTH DAY.

Mrs. Teachum, in the morning, inquired how her scholars did after their walk, and was pleased to hear they were all very well. They then performed their several tasks with much cheerfulness; and, after the school-hours, they were hastening, as usual, to their arbour, when Miss Jenny desired them all to go thither without her, and she would soon follow them; which they readily consented to; but begged her not to deprive them long of the pleasure of her sweet company.

Miss Jenny then went directly into her governess's parlour, and told her that she had some thoughts of reading to her companions a fairy tale, which was also given her by her mamma; and though it was not in such a pompous style, nor so full of wonderful images, as the giant-story; yet she would not venture to read anything of that kind without her permission; but, as she had not absolutely condemned all that sort of writing, she hoped she was not guilty of a fault in asking that permission. Mrs. Teachum, with a gracious smile, told her, that she seemed so thoroughly well to understand the whole force of her Monday night's discourse to her, that she might be trusted almost in anything; and desired her to go and follow her own judgment and inclinations in the amusement of her happy friends. Miss Jenny, overjoyed with this kind condescension in her governess, thanked her, with, a low courtesy, and said, she hoped she should never do anything unworthy of the confidence reposed on her; and, hastening to the arbour, she there found all her little companions quite impatient of this short absence.

Miss Jenny told them, that she had by her a fairy-tale, which, if they liked it, she would read; and, as it had pleased her, she did not doubt but it would give them equal pleasure.

It was the custom now so much amongst them to assent to any proposal that came from Miss Jenny, that they all with one voice desired her to read it; till Miss Polly Suckling said, 'that although she was very unwilling to contradict anything Miss Jenny liked, yet she could not help saying, she thought it would be better if they were to read some true history, from which they might learn something; for she thought fairy-tales were fit only for little children.

Miss Jenny could not help smiling at such an objection's coming from the little dumpling, who was not much above seven years of age; and then said, 'I will tell you a story, my little Polly, of what happened to me whilst I was at home.

'There came into our village, when I was six years old, a man who carried about a raree-show, which all the children of the parish were fond of seeing; but I had taken it into my head, that it was beneath my wisdom to see raree-shows; and therefore would not be persuaded to join my companions to see this sight; and although I had as great an inclination as any of them to see it, yet I avoided it, in order to boast of my own great sense, in that I was above such trifles.

'When my mamma asked me, why I would not see the show, when she had given me leave? I drew up my head, and said, "Indeed I did not like raree-shows. That I had been reading; and I thought that much more worth my while, than to lose my time at such foolish entertainments." My mamma, who saw the cause of my refusing this amusement was only a pretence of being wise, laughed, and said, "She herself had seen it, and it was really very comical and diverting." On hearing this, I was heartily vexed to think I had denied myself a pleasure, which I fancied was beneath me, when I found even my mamma was not above seeing it. This in a great measure cured me of the folly of thinking myself above any innocent amusement. And when I grew older, and more capable of hearing reason, my mamma told me, "She had taken this method of laughing at me, as laughing is the proper manner of treating affectation; which of all things, she said, she would have me carefully avoid; otherwise, whenever I was found out, I should become contemptible."'

Here Miss Jenny ceased speaking; and Miss Polly Suckling, blushing that she had made any objection to what Miss Jenny had proposed, begged her to begin the fairy tale; when just at that instant, Mrs. Teachum, who had been taking a walk in the garden, turned into the arbour to delight herself with a view of her little school united in harmony and love, and Miss Jenny, with great good humour, told her mistress the small contest she had just had with Miss Polly about reading a fairy tale, and the occasion of it. Mrs. Teachum kindly chucking the little dumpling under the chin, said, she had so good an opinion of Miss Jenny, as to answer for her, that she would read nothing to them but what was proper; and added, that she herself would stay and hear this fairy tale which Miss Jenny, on her commands, immediately began.

THE PRINCESS HEBE. A FAIRY TALE.

Above two thousand years ago, there reigned over the kingdom of Tonga, a king, whose name was Abdallah. He was married to a young princess, the daughter of a king of a neighbouring country, whose name was Rousignon. Her beauty and prudence engaged him so far in affection to her, that every hour he could possibly spare from attending the affairs of his kingdom he spent in her apartment. They had a little daughter, to whom they gave the name of Hebe, who was the darling and mutual care of both.

The king was quiet in his dominion, beloved by his subjects, happy in his family, and all his days rolled on in calm content and joy. The king's brother Abdulham was also married to a young princess, named Tropo, who in seven years had brought him no children; and she conceived so mortal a hatred against the queen (for she envied her the happiness of the little Princess Hebe) that she resolved to do her some mischief. It was impossible for her, during the king's lifetime, to vent her malice without being discovered, and therefore she pretended the greatest respect and friendship imaginable for the unsuspecting queen.

Whilst things were in this situation, the king fell into a violent fever, of which he died; and during the time that the queen was in the height of her affliction for him, and could think of nothing but his loss, the Princess Tropo took the opportunity of putting in execution her malicious intentions. She inflamed her husband's passions, by setting forth the meanness of his spirit, in letting a crown be ravished from his head by a female infant, till ambition seized his mind, and he resolved to wield the Tongian sceptre himself. It was very easy to bring this about, for, by his brother's appointment, he was protector of the realm, and guardian to the young princess his niece; and the queen taking him and the princess his wife for her best friends, suspected nothing of their designs, but in a manner gave herself up to their power.

The protector Abdulham, having the whole treasure of the kingdom at his command, was in possession of the means to make all his schemes successful; and the Princess Tropo, by lavishly rewarding the instruments of her treachery, contrived to make it generally believed, that the queen had poisoned her husband, who was so much beloved by his subjects, that the very horror of the action, without any proof of her guilt, raised against the poor unhappy Queen a universal clamour, and a general aversion throughout the whole kingdom. The princess had so well laid her scheme, that the guards were to seize the queen, and convey her to a place of confinement, till she could prove her innocence; which, that she might never be able to do, proper care was taken by procuring sufficient evidence to accuse her on oath; and the Princess Hebe, her daughter, was to be taken from her, and educated under the care of her uncle. But the night before this cruel design was to have been put in execution, a faithful attendant of the queen's, named Loretta, by the assistance of one of the Princess Tropo's confidants (who had long professed himself her lover) discovered the whole secret, of which she immediately informed her royal mistress.

The horrors which filled the queen's mind at the relation of the Princess Tropo's malicious intentions, were inexpressible, and her perturbation so great, that she could not form any scheme that appeared probable to execute for her own preservation. Loretta told her that the person who had given her this timely notice, had also provided a peasant who knew the country, and would meet her at the western gate of the city, and, carrying the young Princess Hebe in his arms, would conduct her to some place of safety; but she must consent to put on a disguise, and escape that very night from the palace, or she would be lost for ever. Horses or mules, she said, it would be impossible to come at without suspicion; therefore she must endeavour (though unused to such fatigue) to travel afoot till she got herself concealed in some cottage from her pursuers, if her enemies should think of endeavouring to find her out. Loretta offered to attend her mistress, but she absolutely forbad her going any farther than to the western gate; where delivering the little Princess Hebe into the arms of the peasant, who was there waiting for them, she reluctantly withdrew.

The good queen, who saw no remedy to this her terrible disgrace, could have borne this barbarous usage without much repining, had she herself been the only sufferer by it; for the loss of the good king her husband so far exceeded all her other misfortunes, that every everything else was trifling in comparison of so dreadful an affliction. But the young Princess Hebe, whom she was accustomed to look on as her greatest blessing, now became to her an object of pity and concern; for, from being heiress to a throne, the poor infant, not yet five years old, was, with her wretched mother, become a vagabond, and knew not whither to fly for protection.

Loretta had prevailed on her royal mistress to take with her a few little necessaries, besides a small picture of the king, and some of her jewels, which the queen contrived to conceal under her night-clothes, in the midst of that hair they were used to adorn, when her loved husband delighted to see it displayed in flowing ringlets round her snowy neck. This lady, during the life of her fond husband, was by his tender care kept from every inclemency of the air, and preserved from every inconvenience that it was possible for human nature to suffer. What then must be her condition now, when through bypaths and thorny ways, she was obliged to fly with all possible speed, to escape the fury of her cruel pursuers: for she too well knew the merciless temper of her enemies, to hope that they would not pursue her with the utmost diligence, especially as she was accompanied by the young Princess Hebe; whose life was the principal cause of their disquiet, and whose destruction they chiefly aimed at.

The honest peasant, who carried the Princess Hebe in his arms, followed the queen's painful steps; and seeing the day begin to break, he begged her, if possible, to hasten on to a wood which was not far off, where it was likely she might find a place of safety. But the afflicted queen, at the sight of the opening morn (which once used to fill her mind with rising joy) burst into a flood of tears, and, quite overcome with grief and fatigue, cast herself on the ground, crying out in the most affecting manner, 'The end of my misfortunes is at hand. My weary limbs will no longer support me. My spirits fail me. In the grave alone must I seek for shelter.' The poor princess, seeing her mother in tears, cast her little arms about her neck, and wept also, though she knew not why.

Whilst she was in this deplorable condition, turning round her head, she saw behind her a little girl, no older in appearance than the Princess Hebe; who, with an amiable and tranquil countenance, begged her to rise and follow her, and she would lead her where she might refresh and repose herself.

The queen was surprised at the manner of speaking of this little child, as she took her to be; but soon thought it was some kind fairy sent to protect her, and was very ready to submit herself to her guidance and protection.

The little fairy (for such indeed was the seeming child who had thus accosted them) ordered the peasant to return back, and said that she would take care of the queen, and her young daughter; and he, knowing her to be the good fairy Sybella, very readily obeyed.

Sybella then striking the ground three times with a little wand, there suddenly rose up before them a neat plain car, and a pair of milk-white horses; and placing the queen with the Princess Hebe in her lap by her side, she drove with excessive swiftness full westward for eight hours; when (just as the sun began to have power enough to make the queen almost faint with the heat and her former fatigue) they arrived at the side of a shady wood; upon entering of which, the fairy made her horses slacken in their speed, and having travelled about a mile and a half, through rows of elms and beech trees, they came to a thick grove of firs, into which there seemed to be no entrance. For there was not any opening to a path, and the underwood consisting chiefly of rose-bushes, white-thorn, eglantine, and other flowering shrubs, was so thick, that it appeared impossible to attempt forcing through them. But alighting out of the car (which immediately disappeared) the fairy (bidding the queen follow her) pushed her way through a large bush of jessamine, whose tender branches gave way for their passage and then closed again, so as to leave no traces of an entrance into this charming grove.

Having gone a little way through an extreme narrow path, they came into an opening (quite surrounded by these firs and sweet underwood) not very large, but in which was contained everything that is necessary towards making life comfortable. At the end of a green meadow was a plain neat house, built more for convenience than beauty, fronting the rising sun; and behind it was a small garden, stored only with fruits and useful herbs. Sybella conducted her guests into this her simple lodging; and as repose was the chief thing necessary for the poor fatigued queen, she prevailed with her to lie down on a couch. Some hours' sound sleep, which her weariness induced, gave her a fresh supply of spirits; the ease and safety from her pursuers, in which she then found herself, made her for a short time tolerably composed; and she begged the favour of knowing to whom she was so greatly obliged for this her happy deliverance; but the fairy seeing her mind too unsettled to give any due attention to what she should say, told her that she would defer the relation of her own life (which was worth her observation) till she had obtained a respite from her own sorrows; and in the meantime, by all manner of obliging ways, she endeavoured to divert and amuse her.

The queen, after a short interval of calmness of mind, occasioned only by her so sudden escape from the terrors of pursuit, returned to her former dejection, and for some time incessantly wept at the dismal thought, that the princess seemed now, by this reverse of fate, to be for ever excluded all hopes of being seated on her father's throne; and, by a strange perverse way of adding to her own grief, she afflicted herself the more, because the little princess was ignorant of her misfortune; and whenever she saw her diverting herself with little childish plays, instead of being pleased with such her innocent amusement, it added to her sorrow, and made her tears gush forth in a larger stream than usual. She could not divert her thoughts from the palace from which she had been driven, to fix them on any other object; nor would her grief suffer her to reflect, that it was possible for the princess to be happy without a crown.

At length time, the great cure of all ills, in some measure abated her Sorrows; her grief began to subside; in spite of herself, the reflection that her misery was only in her own fancy, would sometimes force itself on her mind. She could not avoid seeing, that her little hostess enjoyed as perfect a state of happiness as is possible to attain in this world; that she was free from anxious cares, undisturbed by restless passions, and mistress of all things that could be of any use to make life easy or agreeable. The oftener this reflection presented itself to her thoughts, the more strength it gained; and, at last, she could even bear to think, that her beloved child might be as happy in such a situation, as was her amiable hostess. Her countenance now grew more cheerful; she could take the Princess Hebe in her arms, and thinking the jewels she had preserved would secure her from any fear of want, look on her with delight; and began even to imagine, that her future life might be spent in calm content and pleasure.

As soon as the voice of reason had gained this power over the queen, Sybella told her, that now her bosom was so free from passion, she would relate the history of her life. The queen, overjoyed that her curiosity might now be gratified, begged her not to delay giving her that pleasure one moment; on which our little fairy began in the following manner.

But there Mrs. Teachum told Miss Jenny that the bell rung for dinner; on which she was obliged to break off. But meeting again in the same arbour in the evening, when their good mistress continued to them the favour of her presence, Miss Jenny pursued her story.

THE FAIRY TALE CONTINUED.

'My father,' said the fairy, 'was a magician: he married a lady for love, whose beauty far outshone that of all her neighbours; and by means of that beauty, she had so great an influence over her husband, that she could command the utmost power of his art. But better had it been for her, had that beauty been wanting; for her power only served to make her wish for more, and the gratification of every desire begot a new one, which often it was impossible for her to gratify. My father, though he saw his error in thus indulging her, could not attain steadiness of mind enough to mend it, nor acquire resolution enough to suffer his beloved wife once to grieve or shed a tear to no purpose, though in order to cure her of that folly which made her miserable.

'My grandfather so plainly saw the temper and disposition of his son towards women, that he did not leave him at liberty to dispose of his magic art to any but his posterity, that it might not be in the power of a wife to tease him out of it. But his caution was to very little purpose; for although my mother could not from herself exert any magic power, yet such was her unbounded influence over her husband, that she was sure of success in every attempt to persuade him to gratify her desires. For if every argument she could invent happened to fail, yet the shedding but one tear was a certain method to prevail with him to give up his reason, whatever might be the consequence.

'When my father and mother had been married about a year, she was brought to bed of a daughter, to whom she gave the name of Brunetta. Her first request to my father was, that he would endow this infant with as much beauty as she herself was possessed of, and bestow on her as much of his art as should enable her to succeed in all her designs. My father foresaw the dreadful tendency of granting this request, but said he would give it with this restriction, that she should succeed in all her designs that were not wicked; for, said he, the success of wicked designs always turns out as a punishment to the person so succeeding. In this resolution he held for three days, till my mother (being weak in body after her lying-in) worked herself with her violent passions to such a degree, that the physicians told my father, they despaired of her life, unless some method could be found to make her mind more calm and easy. His fondness for his wife would not suffer him to bear the thoughts of losing her, and the horror with which that apprehension had but for a moment possessed his mind, prevailed with him to bestow on the little Brunetta (though foreseeing it would make her miserable) the fatal gift in its full extent. But one restriction it was out of his power to take off, namely, that all wicked designs ever could and should be rendered ineffectual by the virtue and perseverance of those against whom they were intended, if they in a proper manner exerted that virtue.

'I was born in two years after Brunetta, and was called Sybella: but my mother was so taken up with her darling Brunetta, that she gave herself not the least concern about me; and I was left wholly to the care of my father. In order to make the gift she had extorted from her fond husband as fatal as possible to her favourite child, she took care in her education (by endeavouring to cultivate in her the spirit of revenge and malice against those who had in the least degree offended her) to turn her mind to all manner of mischief; by which means she lived in a continual passion.

'My father, as soon as I was old enough to hearken to reason, told me of the gift he had conferred on my sister; said he could not retract it; and therefore, if she had any mischievous designs against me, they must in some measure succeed; but she would endow me with a power superior to this gift of my sister's, and likewise superior to any thing else that he was able to bestow, which was strength and constancy of mind enough to bear patiently any injuries I might receive; and this was a strength, he said, which would not decay, but rather increase, by every new exercise of it; and, to secure me in the possession of this gift, he likewise gave me a perfect knowledge of the true value of everything around me, by which means I might learn, whatever outward accidents befell me, not to lose the greatest blessing in this world, namely, a calm and contented mind. He taught me so well my duty, that I cheerfully obeyed my mother in all things, though she seldom gave me a kind word, or even a kind look; for my spiteful sister was always telling some lies to make her angry with me. But my heart overflowed with gratitude to my father, that he would give me leave to love him, whilst he instructed me that it was my duty to pay him the most strict obedience.

'Brunetta was daily encouraged by her mother to use me ill, and chiefly because my father loved me; and although she succeeded in all her designs of revenge on me, yet was she very uneasy, because she could not take away the cheerfulness of my mind; for I bore with patience whatever happened to me: and she would often say, "must I with all my beauty, power, and wisdom (for so she called her low cunning) be suffering perpetual uneasiness? and shall you, who have neither beauty, power, nor wisdom, pretend to be happy and cheerful?" Then would she cry and stamp, and rave like a mad creature, and set her invention at work to make my mother beat me, or lock me up, or take from me some of my best clothes to give to her; yet still could not her power extend to vex my mind: and this used to throw her again into such passions, as weakened her health, and greatly impaired her so much boasted beauty.

'In this manner we lived, till on a certain day, after Brunetta had been in one of her rages with me for nothing, my father came in and chid her for it; which, when my mother heard, she threw herself into such a violent passion, that her husband could not pacify her. And, being big with child, the convulsions, caused by her passions, brought her to her grave. Thus my father lost her, by the same uncontrollable excesses, the fatal effects of which he had before ruined his daughter to preserve her from. He did not long survive her; but, before he died, gave me a little wand, which, by striking three times on the ground, he said, would at any time produce me any necessary or convenience of life, which I really wanted, either for myself, or the assistance of others; and this he gave me, because he was very sensible, he said, that as soon as he was dead, my sister would never rest till she had got from me both his castle, and everything that I had belonging to me, in it. "But," continued he, "whenever you are driven from thence, bend your course directly into the pleasant wood Ardella; there strike with your wand, and everything you want, will be provided for you. But keep this wand a profound secret, or Brunetta will get it from you; and then (though you can never, while you preserve your patience, be unhappy) you will not have it in your power to be of so much use as you would wish to be, to those who shall stand in need of your assistance." Saying these words, he expired, as I kneeled by his bedside, attending his last commands, and bewailing the loss of so good a father.

'In the midst of this our distress, we sent to my Uncle Sochus, my father's brother, to come to us, and to assist us in an equal division of my deceased father's effects; but my sister soon contrived to make him believe, that I was the wickedest girl alive, and had always set my father against her by my art, which she said I pretended to call my wisdom; and by several handsome presents she soon persuaded him (for he did not care a farthing for either of us) to join with her in saying, that, as she was the eldest sister, she had a full right to the castle, and everything in it; but she told me I was very welcome to stay there, and live with her, if I pleased; and while I behaved myself well, she should be very glad of my company.

'As it was natural for me to love every one that would give me leave to love them, I was quite overjoyed at this kind offer of my sister's, and never once thought on the treachery she had so lately been guilty of; and I have since reflected, that happy was it for me, that passion was so much uppermost with her, that she could not execute any plot, that required a dissimulation of any long continuance; for had her good humour lasted but one four-and-twenty hours, it is very probable that I should have opened my whole heart to her; should have endeavoured to have begun a friendship with her, and perhaps have betrayed the secret of my wand; but just as it was sunset, she came into the room where I was, in the most violent passion in the world, accusing me to my uncle of ingratitude to her great generosity, in suffering me to live in her castle. She said, "that she had found me out, and that my crimes were of the blackest dye," although she would not tell me either what they were, or who were my accusers. She would not give me leave to speak, either to ask what my offence was, or to justify my innocence; and I plainly perceived, that her pretended kindness was only designed to make my disappointment the greater; and that she was now determined to find me guilty, whether I pleaded, or not. And after she had raved on for some time, she said to me with a sneer, "Since you have always boasted of your calm and contented mind, you may now try to be contented this night with the softness of the grass for your bed; for here in my castle you shall not stay one moment longer." And so saying, she and my uncle led me to the outer court, and thrusting me with all their force from them, they shut up the gates, bolting and barring them as close as if to keep out a giant; and left me, at that time of night, friendless, and, as they thought, destitute of any kind of support.

'I then remembered my dear father's last words, and made what haste I could to this wood, which is not above a mile distant from the castle; and being, as I thought, about the middle of it, I struck three times with my wand, and immediately up rose this grove of trees, which you see, this house, and all the other conveniences, which I now enjoy; and getting that very night into this my plain and easy bed, I enjoyed as sweet a repose as ever I did in my life, only delayed, indeed, a short time, by a few sighs, for the loss of so good a parent, and the unhappy state of a self-tormented sister, whose slumbers (I fear) on a bed of down, were more restless and interrupted that night than mine would have been, even had not my father's present of the wand prevented me from the necessity of using the bed of grass, which she, in her wrath, allotted me. In this grove, which I call Placid Grove, is contained all that I want; and it is so well secured from any invaders, by the thick briars and thorns which surround it, having no entrance but through that tender jessamine, that I live in no apprehensions of any disturbance, though so near my sister's castle. But once, indeed, she came with a large train, and, whilst I was asleep, set fire to the trees all around me; and waking, I found myself almost suffocated with smoke, and the flames had reached one part of my House. I started from my bed, and striking on the ground three times with my wand, there came such a quantity of water from the heavens, as soon extinguished the fire; and the next morning, by again having recourse to my wand, all things grew up into their convenient and proper order. When my sister Brunetta found that I had such a supernatural power at my command, though she knew not what it was, she desisted from ever attempting any more by force to disturb me; and now only uses all sorts of arts and contrivances to deceive me, or any persons whom I would wish to secure. One of my father's daily lessons to me was, that I should never omit any one day of my life endeavouring to be as serviceable as I possibly could to any person in distress. And I daily wander, as far as my feet will carry me, in search of any such, and hither I invite them to peace and calm contentment. But my father added also this command, that I should never endeavour doing any farther good to those whom adversity had not taught to hearken to the voice of reason, enough to enable them so to conquer their passions as not to think themselves miserable in a safe retreat from noise and confusion. This was the reason I could not gratify you in relating the history of my life, whilst you gave way to raging passions, which only serve to blind your eyes, and shut your ears from truth. But now, great queen (for I know your state, from what you vented in your grief), I am ready to endow this little princess with any gift in my power, that I know will tend really to her good; and I hope your experience of the world has made you too reasonable to require any other.'

The queen considered a little while, and then desired Sybella to endow the princess with that only wisdom which would enable her to see and follow what was her own true good, to know the value of everything around her, and to be sensible that following the paths of goodness and performing her duty was the only road to content and happiness.

Sybella was overjoyed at the queen's request, and immediately granted it, only telling the Princess Hebe, that it was absolutely necessary towards the attainment of this great blessing, that she should entirely obey the queen her mother, without ever pretending to examine her commands; for 'true obedience (said she) consists in submission; and when we pretend to choose what commands are proper and fit for us, we don't obey, but set up our own wisdom in opposition to our governors—this, my dear Hebe, you must be very careful of avoiding, if you would be happy.' She then cautioned her against giving way to the persuasions of any of the young shepherdesses thereabouts, who would endeavour to allure her to disobedience, by striving to raise in her mind a desire of thinking herself wise, whilst they were tearing from her what was indeed true wisdom. 'For (said Sybella) my sister Brunetta, who lives in the castle she drove me from (about a mile from this wood) endows young shepherdesses with great beauty, and everything that is in appearance amiable, and likely to persuade, in order to allure away and make wretched, those persons I would preserve: and all the wisdom with which I have endowed the Princess Hebe will not prevent her falling into my sister's snares, if she gives the least way to temptation; for my father's gift to Brunetta, in her infancy, enables her (as I told you) to succeed in all her designs, except they are resisted by the virtue of the person she is practising against. Many poor wretches has my sister already decoyed away from me, whom she now keeps in her castle; where they live in splendor and seeming joy, but in real misery, from perpetual jars and tumults, railed by envy, malice, and all the train of tumultuous and tormenting passions.'

The Princess Hebe said, she doubted not but she should be able to withstand any of Brunetta's temptations. Her mother interrupting her, cried out, 'Oh, my dear child, though you are endowed with wisdom enough to direct you in the way to virtue, yet if you grow conceited and proud of that wisdom, and fancy yourself above temptation, it will lead you into the worst of all evils.' Here the fairy interposed, and told the Princess Hebe, that if she would always carefully observe and obey her mother, who had learned wisdom in that best school, adversity, she would then, indeed, be able to withstand and overcome every temptation, and would likewise be happy herself, and able to dispense happiness to all around her. Nothing was omitted by the fairy to make this retirement agreeable to her royal guests; and they had now passed near seven years in this delightful grove, in perfect peace and tranquillity; when one evening, as they were walking in the pleasant wood which surrounded their habitation, they espied under the shade, and leaning against the bark of a large oak, a poor old man, whose limbs were withered and decayed, and whose eyes were hollow, and sunk with age and misery. They stopped as soon as they saw him, and heard him in the anguish of his heart, with a loud groan, utter these words: 'When will my sorrows end? Where shall I find the good fairy Sybella?' The fairy immediately begged to know his business with her; and said, if his sorrows would end on finding Sybella, he might set his heart at ease; for she stood now before him, and ready to serve him, if his distresses were such as would admit of relief, and he could prove himself worthy of her friendship. The old Man appeared greatly overjoyed at having found the fairy, and began the following story:

'I live from hence a thousand leagues. All this tiresome way have I come in search of you. My whole life has been spent in amassing wealth, to enrich one only son, whom I doted on to distraction. It is now five years since I have given him up all the riches I had laboured to get, only to make him happy. But, alas how am I disappointed! His wealth enables him to command whatever this world produces; and yet the poorest wretch that begs his bread cannot be more miserable. He spends his days in riot and luxury; has more slaves and attendants than wait in the palace of a prince; and still he sighs from morning till night, because, he says, there is nothing in this world worth living for. All his dainties only sate his palate, and grow irksome to his sight. He daily changes his opinion of what is pleasure; and, on the trial, finds none that he can call such; and then falls to sighing again, for the emptiness of all that he has enjoyed. So that, instead of being my delight, and the comfort of my old age, sleepless nights, and anxious days, are all the rewards of my past labours for him. But I have had many visions and dreams to admonish me, that if I would venture with my old frame to travel hither a-foot in search of the fairy Sybella, she had a glass, which if she showed him, he would be cured of this dreadful melancholy, and I have borne the labour and fatigue of coming this long tiresome way, that I may not breathe my last with the agonizing reflection, that all the labours of my life have been thrown away. But what shall I say to engage you to go with me? Can riches tempt, or praise allure you?'

'No, (answered the fairy) neither of them has power to move me; but I compassionate your age; and if I thought I could succeed, would not refuse you. The glass which I shall bid him look in, will show him his inward self; but if he will not open both his eyes and heart enough to truth, to let him understand, that the pleasures he pursues not only are not but cannot be satisfactory, I can be of no sort of service to him. And know, old man, that the punishment you now feel is the natural result of your not having taught him this from his infancy; for, instead of heaping up wealth, to allure him to seek for happiness from such deceitful means, you should have taught him, that the only path to it was to be virtuous and good.'

The old man said, he heartily repented of his conduct, and on his knees so fervently implored Sybella's assistance, that at last she consented to go with him. Then striking on the ground three times with her wand, the car and horses rose up, and placing the old Man by her, after taking leave of the queen, and begging the Princess Hebe to be careful to guard against all temptations to disobedience, she set out on her journey.

It being now come to the latest hour that Mrs. Teachum thought proper for her little scholars to stay out in the air, she told Miss Jenny that she must defer reading the remaining part of her story till the next day. Miss Jenny always with great cheerfulness obeyed her governess, and immediately left off reading; and said she was ready to attend her; and the whole company rose up to follow her.

Mrs. Teachum had so much judgment, that, perceiving such a ready obedience to all her commands, she now endeavoured, by all means she could think of; to make her scholars throw off that reserve before her, which must ever make it uneasy to them for her ever to be present whilst they were following their innocent diversions; for such was the understanding of this good woman, that she could keep up the authority of the governess in her school, yet at times become the companion of her scholars. And as she now saw, by their good behaviour, they deserved that indulgence, she took the little dumpling by the hand, and, followed by the rest, walked towards the house, and discoursed familiarly with them the rest of the evening, concerning all their past amusements.

SATURDAY. THE SIXTH DAY.

It was the custom on Saturdays to have no school in the afternoon, and it being also their writing day from morning-school till dinner, Mrs. Teachum, knowing how eager Miss Jenny's hearers were for the rest of the story, accompanied them into the arbour, early in the afternoon, when Miss Jenny went on as follows:

THE FAIRY TALE CONTINUED.

The queen and the Princess Hebe remained, by the good fairy's desire, in her habitation during her absence. They spent their time in serenity and content; the princess daily improving herself in wisdom and goodness, by hearkening to her mother's instructions, and obeying all her commands, and the queen in studying what would be of most use to her child. She had now forgot her throne and palace, and desired nothing for her, than her present peaceful retreat. One morning, as they were sitting in a little arbour at the corner of a pleasant meadow, on a sudden they heard a voice, much sweeter than they had ever heard, warble through the following song:

A SONG.

Virtue, soft balm of every woe,   Of ev'ry grief the cure,   'Tis thou alone that canst best bestow   Pleasures unmix'd and pure.   The shady wood, the verdant mead,   Are Virtue's flow'ry road;   Nor painful are the steps which lead   To her divine abode.   'Tis not in palaces of halls, She or their train appear;   Far off she flies from pompous walls;   Virtue and Peace dwell here.

The queen was all attention, and at the end of the song she gazed around her, in hopes of seeing the person whose enchanting voice she had been so eagerly listening to, when she espied a young shepherdess, not much older than the Princess Hebe, but possessed of such uncommon and dazzling beauty, that it was some time before she could disengage her eyes from so agreeable an object. As soon as the young shepherdess found herself observed, she seemed modestly to offer to withdraw; but the queen begged her not to go till she had informed them who she was, that, with such a commanding aspect, had so much engaged them in her favour.

The shepherdess coming forward, with a bashful blush, and profound obedience, answered, that her name was Rozella, and she was the daughter of a neighbouring shepherd and shepherdess, who lived about a quarter of a mile from thence; and, to confess the truth, she had wandered thither, in hopes of seeing the young stranger, whose fame for beauty and wisdom had filled all that country round.

The Princess Hebe, well knowing of whom she spoke, conceived from that moment such an inclination fur her acquaintance, that she begged her to stay and spend that whole day with them in Placid Grove. Here the queen frowned upon her, for she had, by the fairy's desire, charged her never to bring any one, without her permission, into that peaceful grove.

The young Rozella answered, that nothing could be more agreeable to her inclinations; but she must be at home by noon, for so in the morning had her father commanded her, and never yet in her life had she either disputed or disobeyed her parent's commands. Here the young princess looked on her mother with eyes expressive of her joy at finding a companion, which she, and even the fairy herself, could not disapprove.

When Rozella took her leave, she begged the favour that the little Hebe (for so she called her, not knowing her to be a princess) might come to her father's small cottage, and there partake such homely fare as it afforded; a welcome, she said, she could insure her; and though poor, yet from the honesty of her parents, who would be proud to entertain so rare a beauty, she was certain no sort of harm could happen to the pretty Hebe, from such a friendly visit; and she would be in the same place again tomorrow, to meet her, in hopes, as she said, to conduct her to her humble habitation.

When Rozella was gone, the queen, though highly possessed in her favour, both by her beauty and modest behaviour, yet pondered some time on the thought, whether or no she was a fit companion for her daughter. She remembered what Sybella had told her, concerning Brunetta's adorning young shepherdesses with beauty, and other excellences, only to enable them the better to allure and entice others into wickedness. Rozella's beginning her acquaintance too with the princess, by flattery, had no good aspect; and the sudden effect it had upon her, so as to make her forget, or wilfully disobey, her commands, by inviting Rozella to Placid Grove, were circumstances which greatly alarmed her. But, by the repeated entreaties of the princess, she gave her consent that she should meet Rozella the next day, and walk with her in that meadow, and in the wood, but upon no account should she go home with her, or bring Rozella back with her. The queen then, in gentle terms, chid the princess for her invitation to the young shepherdess, which was contrary to an absolute command; and said, 'You must, my dear Hebe, be very careful to guard yourself extremely well against those temptations which wear the face of virtue. I know that your sudden affection to this apparent good girl, and your desire of her company, to partake with you the innocent pleasures of this happy place, arise from a good disposition; but where the indulgence of the most laudable passion, even benevolence and compassion itself, interferes with, or runs counter to your duty, you must endeavour to suppress it, or it will fare with you, as it did with that hen, who, thinking that she heard the voice of a little duckling in distress, flew from her young ones, to go and give it assistance, and following the cry, came at last to a hedge, out of which jumped a subtle and wicked fox, who had made that noise to deceive her, and devoured her in an instant. A kite at the same time, taking advantage of her absence, carried away, one by one, all her little innocent brood, robbed of that parent who should have been their protector.' The princess promised her mother that she would punctually obey all her commands, and be very watchful and observant of everything Rozella said and did, till she had approved herself worthy of her confidence and friendship.

The queen the next morning renewed her injunctions to her daughter, that she should by no means go farther out of the wood than into the meadow, where she was to meet Rozella, and that she should give her a faithful account of all that should pass between them.

They met according to appointment, and the princess brought home so good an account of their conversation, which the queen imagined would help to improve, rather than seduce her child, that she indulged her in the same pleasure as often as she asked it. They passed some hours every day in walking round that delightful wood, in which were many small green meadows, with little rivulets running through them, on the banks of which, covered with primroses and violets, Rozella, by the side of her sweet companion, used to sing the most enchanting songs in the world: the words were chiefly in praise of innocence and a country life.

The princess came home every day more and more charmed with her young shepherdess, and recounted, as near as she could remember, every word that had passed between them. The queen very highly approved of their manner of amusing themselves; but again enjoined her to omit nothing that passed in conversation, especially if it had the least tendency towards alluring her from her duty.

One day, as the princess Hebe and Rozella were walking alone, and talking, as usual, of their own happy state, and the princess was declaring how much her own happiness was owing to her thorough obedience to her mother, Rozella, with a tone of voice as half in jest, said, 'But don't you think, my little Hebe, that if I take a very great pleasure in any thing that will do me no hurt, though it is forbidden, I may disobey my parents in enjoying it, provided I don't tell them of it to vex them with the thought that I have disobeyed them? And then, my dear, what harm is done?'

'Great harm (answered the princess, looking grave and half angry): I am ashamed to hear you talk so, Rozella. Are you not guilty of treachery, as well as disobedience? Neither ought you to determine that no harm is done, because you do not feel the immediate effects of your transgression; for the consequence may be out of our narrow inexperienced view; and I have been taught whenever my mother lays any commands on me, to take it for granted, she has some reason for so doing; and I obey her, without examining what those reasons are; otherwise, it would not be obeying her, but setting up my own wisdom, and doing what she bid me, only when I thought proper.'

They held a long argument on this head, in which Rozella made use of many a fallacy to prove her point; but the princess, as she had not yet departed from Truth, nor failed in her duty, could not be imposed upon. Rozella, seeing every attempt to persuade her was in vain, turned all her past discourse into a jest; said she had only a mind to try her; and was overjoyed to find her so steady in the cause of truth and virtue. The princess resumed her usual cheerfulness and good humour. Rozella sung her a song in praise of constancy of mind; and they passed the rest of the time they stayed together, as they used to do.

But, just before they parted, Rozella begged she would not tell her mother of the first part of the conversation that had passed between them. The princess replied, that it would be breaking through one of her mother's commands, and therefore she dared not grant her request. Then, said Rozella, 'Here I must for ever part with my dear little Hebe. Your mother, not knowing the manner in which I spoke, will have an ill opinion of me, and will never trust you again in my company. Thus will you be torn from me; and loss will be irreparable.' These words she accompanied with a flood of tears, and such little tendernesses, as quite melted the princess into tears also. But she still said, that she could not dare to conceal from her mother anything that had happened, though she could not but own, she believed their separation would be the consequence. 'Well then (cried Rozella) I will endeavour to be contented, as our separation will give you less pain than what you call this mighty breach of your duty: and though I would willingly undergo almost any torments that could be invented, rather than be debarred one moment the company of my dearest Hebe, yet I will not expect that she should suffer the smallest degree of pain, or uneasiness, to save me from losing what is the whole pleasure of my life.'

The princess could not bear the thought of appearing ungrateful to such a warm friendship as Rozella expressed; and, without farther hesitation, promised to conceal what she had said, and to undergo anything, rather than lose so amiable a friend.

After this they parted. But when the princess entered the Grove, she did not, as usual, run with haste and joy into the presence of her indulgent mother; for her mind was disturbed: she felt a conscious shame on seeing her, and turned away her face, as wanting to shun the piercing look of that eye, which she imagined would see the secret lurking in her bosom. Her mother observed with concern her downcast look, and want of cheerfulness. And asking her what was the matter, she answered, her walk had fatigued her, and she begged early to retire to rest. Her kind mother consented; but little rest had the poor princess that whole night, for the pain of having her mind touched with guilt, and the fear she was under of losing her dear companion, kept her thoughts in one continued tumult and confusion. The fairy's gift now became her curse; for the power of seeing what was right, as she had acted contrary to her knowledge, only tormented her.

She hastened the next morning to meet Rozella, and told her all that had passed in her own mind the preceding night; declaring that she would not pass such another for the whole world; but yet would not dispense with her promise to her, without her consent; and therefore came to ask her leave to acquaint her good mother with all that had passed: 'For (said she) my dear Rozella, we must, if we would be happy, do always what is right, and trust for the consequences.' Here Rozella drew her features into the most contemptuous sneer imaginable, and said, 'Pray what are all these mighty pains you have suffered? Are they not owing only to your want of sense enough to know, that you can do your mother no harm, by concealing from her this, or anything else that will vex her? and, my dear girl (continued she) when you have once entered into this way of thinking, and have put this blind duty out of your head, you will spend no more such restless nights, which you must see was entirely owing to your own imaginations.'

This startled the princess to such a degree, that she was breaking from her, but, putting on a more tender air, Rozella cried, 'And can you then, my dear Hebe, determine to give me up for such a trifling consideration?' Then raising her voice again, in a haughty manner, she said, 'I ought to despise and laugh at you for your folly, or at best pity your ignorance, rather than offer a sincere friendship to one so undeserving.'

The princess, having once swerved from her duty, was now in the power of every passion that should attack her.

Pride and indignation, at the thought of being despised, bore more sway with her, than either her duty or affection to her fond mother; and she was now determined, she said, to think for herself, and make use of her own understanding, which she was convinced would always teach her what was right. Upon this Rozella took her by the hand, and, with tears of joy, said, 'Now, my dearest girl, you are really wise, and cannot therefore (according to your own rule) fail of being happy. But to show that you are in earnest in this resolution, you shall this morning go home with me to my father's cot; it is not so far off, but you will be back by the time your mother expects you; and as that will be obeying the chief command, it is but concealing from her the thing that would vex her, and there will be no harm done.' Here a ray of truth broke in upon our young princess; but as a false shame, and fear of being laughed at, had now got possession of her, she, with a soft sigh, consented to the proposal.

Rozella led the way. But just as they were turning round the walk, which leads out of the wood, a large serpent darted from one side out of a thicket, directly between them, and turning its hissing mouth towards the princess, as seeming to make after her, she fled hastily back, and ran with all her speed towards the grove, and panting for breath, flew into the arms of her ever kind protectress.

Her mother was vastly terrified to see her tremble, and look so pale; and as soon as she was a little recovered, asked her the occasion of her fright, and added (with tears running down her cheeks) 'I am afraid, my dear Hebe, some sad disaster has befallen you, for, indeed, my child, I but too plainly saw last night—'

Here the princess was so struck with true shame and confusion, for her past behaviour, that she fell down upon her knees, confessed the whole truth, and implored forgiveness for her fault.

The queen kindly raised her up, kissed and forgave her. 'I am overjoyed, my dear child (said she) at this your sweet repentance, though the effect of mere accident, as it appears but sent, without doubt, by some good fairy, to save you from destruction; and I hope you are thoroughly convinced, that the serpent which drove you home, was not half so dangerous as the false Rozella.'

The princess answered, that she was thoroughly sensible of the dangers she had avoided, and hoped she never should again, by her own folly and wickedness, deserve to be exposed to the danger from which she had so lately escaped.

Some days passed, without the princess's offering to stir out of the grove; and in that time she gave a willing and patient ear to all her mother's instructions, and seemed thoroughly sensible of the great deliverance she had lately experienced. But yet there appeared in her countenance an uneasiness, which the queen wishing to remove, asked her the cause of.

'It is, dear madam,' answered the princess, 'because I have not yet had it in my power to convince you of my repentance, which (though I know it to be sincere) you have had no proof of, but in words only; and, indeed, my heart longs for an occasion to show you, that I am now able to resist any allurement which would tempt me from my duty; and I cannot be easy till you have given me an opportunity of showing you the firmness of my resolution; and if you will give me leave to take a walk in the wood alone, this evening, I shall return to you with pleasure, and will promise not to exceed any bounds that you shall prescribe.'

The queen was not much pleased with this request; but the princess was so earnest with her to grant it, that she could not well refuse, without seeming to suspect her sincerity; which she did not, but only feared for her safety, and, giving her a strict charge, not to stir a step out of the wood, or to speak to the false Rozella, if she came in her way, she reluctantly gave her consent.

The princess walked through all the flowery labyrinths, in which she had so often strayed with Rozella; but she was so shocked with the thoughts of her wickedness, that she hardly gave a sigh for the loss of a companion once so dear to her; and as a proof that her repentance was sincere, though she heard Rozella singing in an arbour (purposely perhaps to decoy her) she turned away without the least emotion, and went quite to the other side of the wood; where looking into the meadow, in which she first beheld that false friend, she saw a girl about her own age, leaning against a tree, and crying most bitterly. But the moment she came in sight, the young shepherdess (for such by her dress she appeared to be) cried out, 'O help, dear young lady, help me; for I am tied here to this tree, by the spiteful contrivance of a wicked young shepherdess called Rozella: my hands too, you see, are bound behind me, so that I cannot myself unloose the knot; and if I am not released, here must I lie all night and my wretched parents will break their hearts, for fear some sad accident should have befallen their only child, their poor unhappy Florimel!'

The Princess, hearing her speak of Rozella in that manner, had no suspicion of her being one of that false girl's deluding companions; but rather thought that she was a fellow-sufferer with herself; and therefore, without any consideration of the bounds prescribed, she hastened to relieve her, and even thought that she should have great pleasure in telling her mother, that she had saved a poor young shepherdess from Rozella's malice, and restored her to her fond parents. But as soon as she had unloosed the girl from the tree, and unbound her hands, instead of receiving thanks for what she had done, the wicked Florimel burst into a laugh, and suddenly snatching from the Princess Hebe's side her father's picture, which she always wore hanging in a ribbon, she ran away with it, as fast as she could, over the meadow.

The Princess was so astonished at this strange piece of ingratitude and treachery, and was so alarmed for fear of losing what she knew her mother so highly valued, that hardly knowing what she was about, she pursued Florimel with all her speed, begging and entreating her not to bereave her so basely and ungratefully of that picture, which she would not part with for the world: but it was all to no purpose for Florimel continued her flight, and the princess her pursuit, till they arrived at Brunetta's castle-gate; where the fairy herself appeared dressed and adorned in the most becoming manner, and, with the most bewitching smile that can come from dazzling beauty, invited the princess to enter her castle (into which Florimel was run to hide herself) and promised her, on that condition, to make the idle girl restore the picture.

It was now so late, that it was impossible for the princess to think of returning home that night; and the pleasing address of Brunetta, together with the hopes of having her picture restored, soon prevailed with her to accept of the fairy's invitation.

The castle glittered with gaudy furniture; sweet music was heard in every room; the whole company, who were all of the most beautiful forms that could be conceived, strove who should be most obliging to this their new guest. They omitted nothing that could amuse and delight the senses. And the Princess Hebe was so entranced with joy and rapture, that she had not time for thought, or for the least serious reflection; and she now began to think, that she had attained the highest happiness upon earth.

After they had kept her three days in this round of pleasure and delight, they began to pull of the mask; nothing was heard but quarrels, jars, and galling speeches. Instead of sweet music, the apartments were filled with screams and howling; for every one giving way to the most outrageous passions, they were always doing each other some malicious turn, and only universal horror and confusion reigned.

The princess was hated by all, and was often asked, with insulting sneers, why she did not return to her peaceful grove, and condescending mother? But her mind having been thus turned aside from what was right, could not bear the thoughts of returning; and though by her daily tears, she showed her repentance, shame prevented her return: but this again was not the right sort of shame; for then she would humbly have taken the punishment due to her crime; and it was rather a stubborn pride, which, as she knew herself so highly to blame, would not give her leave to suffer the confusion of again confessing her fault; and till she could bring herself to such a state of mind, there was no remedy for her misery.

Just as Miss Jenny had read these words, Mrs. Teachum remembering some orders necessary to give in her family, left them, but bid them go on, saying she would return again in a quarter of an hour. But she was no sooner gone from them, than our little company, hearing the sound of trumpets and kettle-drums, which seemed to be playing at some little distance from Mrs. Teachum's house, suddenly started from their seats, running directly to the terrace; and, looking over the garden wall, they saw a troop of soldiers riding by, with these instruments of music playing before them.

They were highly delighted with the gallant and splendid appearance of these soldiers, and watched them till they were out of sight, and were then returning to their arbour, where Miss Jenny had been reading; but Miss Nanny Spruce espied another such troop coming out of the lane from whence the first had issued, and cried out, 'O! here is another fine sight; let us stay, and see these go by too.' 'Indeed (said Miss Dolly Friendly) I am in such pain for the poor princess Hebe, while she is in that sad castle, that I had rather hear how she escaped (for that I hope she will) than see all the soldiers in the world; and besides, it is but seeing the same thing we have just looked at before.' Here some were for staying, and others for going back; but as Miss Dolly's party was the strongest, the few were ashamed to avow their inclinations; and they were returning to the arbour, when they met Mrs. Teachum, who informed them their dancing master was just arrived, and they must attend him; but in the evening they might finish their story.

They were so curious (and especially Miss Dolly Friendly) to know what was to become of the princess, that they could have wished not to have been interrupted; but yet, without one word of answer, they complied with what their governess thought most proper; and in the evening, hastening to their arbour, Mrs. Teachum herself being present, Miss Jenny went on in the following manner:

THE FAIRY TALE CONTINUED.

The queen, in the meantime, suffered for the loss of her child more than words can express, till the good fairy Sybella returned. The queen burst into tears at the sight of her; but the fairy immediately cried out, 'You may spare yourself, my royal guest, the pain of relating what has happened. I know it all; for that old man, whom I took such pity on, was a phantom, raised by Brunetta, to allure me hence, in order to have an opportunity, in my absence, of seducing the princess from her duty. She knew nothing but a probable story could impose on me, and therefore raised that story of the misery of the old man's son (from motives which too often, indeed, cause the misery of mortals); as knowing I should think it my duty to do what I could to relieve such a wretch. I will not tell you all my journey, nor what I have gone through. I know your mind is at present too much fixed on the princess, to attend to such a relation I'll only tell you what concerns yourself. When the phantom found, that by no distress he could perturb my mind, he said he was obliged to tell the truth, what was the intention of my being deluded from home, and what had happened since; and then vanished away.' Here the fairy related to the queen everything that had happened to the princess, as has already been written; and concluded with saying, that she would wander about the castle walls (for Brunetta had no power over her); and if she could get a sight of the princess, she would endeavour to bring her to a true sense of her fault, and then she might again be restored to happiness.

The queen blessed the fairy for her goodness; and it was not long before Sybella's continual assiduity got her a sight of the princess; for she often wandered a little way towards that wood she had once so much delighted in, but never could bring herself to enter into it: the thought of seeing her injured mother made her start back, and run half wild into the fatal castle. Rozella used frequently to throw herself in her way; and on hearing her sighs, and seeing her tears, would burst into a sneering laugh at her folly; to avoid which laugh, the poor princess first suffered herself to throw off all her principles of goodness and obedience, and was now fallen into the very contempt she so much dreaded.

The first time the fairy got a sight of her, she called to her with the most friendly voice; but the princess, stung to the soul with the sight of her, fled away, and did not venture out again in several days. The kind Sybella began almost to despair of regaining her lost child; but never failed walking round the castle many hours every day. And one evening, just before the sun set, she heard within the gates a loud tumultuous noise, but more like riotous mirth, than either the voice either of rage or anger; and immediately she saw the princess rush out at the gate, and about a dozen girls, laughing and shouting, running after her. The poor princess flew with all her speed till she came to a little arbour, just by the side of the wood; and her pursuers, as they intended only to tease her, did not follow her very close; but, as soon as they lost sight of her, turned all back again to the castle.

Sybella went directly into the arbour, where she found the little trembler prostrate on the ground, crying and sobbing as if her heart was breaking. The fairy seized her hand, and would not let her go till she had prevailed with her to return to the Placid Grove, to throw herself once more at her mother's feet, assuring her, that nothing but this humble state of mind could cure her misery and restore her wonted peace.

The queen was filled with the highest joy to see her child; but restrained herself so much, that she showed not the least sign of it, till she had seen her some time prostrate at her feet, and had heard her with tears properly confess, and ask pardon for, all her faults. She then raised, and once more forgave her; but told her that she must learn more humility and distrust of herself, before she should again expect to be trusted.

The princess answered not, but with a modest downcast look which expressed her concern and true repentance, and in a short time recovered her former peace of mind; and as she never afterwards disobeyed her indulgent mother, she daily increased in wisdom and goodness.

After having lived on in the most innocent and peaceful manner for three years (the princess being just turned of eighteen years old) the fairy told the queen that she would now tell her some news of her kingdom, which she had heard in her journey; namely, that her sister-in-law was dead, and her brother-in-law had made proclamation throughout the kingdom, of great rewards to any one who should produce the queen and the Princess Hebe, whom he would immediately reinstate on the throne.

The Princess Hebe was by when she related this, and said she begged to lead a private life, and never more be exposed to the temptation of entering into vice, for which she already had so severely smarted.

The fairy told her, that, since she doubted herself, she was now fit to be trusted; for, said she, 'I did not like your being so sure of resisting temptation, when first I conferred on you the gift of wisdom. But you will, my princess, if you take the crown, have an opportunity of doing so much good, that, if you continue virtuous, you will have perpetual pleasures; for power, if made a right use of, is indeed a very great blessing.'

The princess answered, that if the queen, her mother, thought it her duty to take the crown, she would cheerfully submit, though a private life would be otherwise her choice.

The queen replied, that she did not blame her for choosing a private life; but she thought she could not innocently refuse the power that would give her such opportunities of doing good, and making others happy; since, by that refusal, the power might fall into hands that would make an ill use of it.

After this conversation, they got into the same car in which they travelled to the wood of Ardella; arrived safely at the city of Algorada; and the Princess Hebe was seated, with universal consent, on her father's throne; where she and her people were reciprocally happy, by her great wisdom and prudence; and the queen-mother spent the remainder of her days in peace and joy, to see her beloved daughter prove a blessing to such numbers of human creatures; whilst she herself enjoyed that only true content and happiness this world can produce; namely, a peaceful conscience, and a quiet mind.

When Miss Jenny had finished her story, Mrs. Teachum left them for the present, that they might with the utmost freedom make their own observations; for she knew she should be acquainted with all their sentiments from Miss Jenny afterwards.

The little hearts of all the company were swelled with joy, in that the Princess Hebe was at last made happy; for hope and fear had each by turns possessed their bosoms for the fate of the little princess; and Miss Dolly Friendly said, that Rozella's artful manner was enough to have drawn in the wisest girl into her snares; and she did not see how it was possible for the Princess Hebe to withstand it, especially when she cried for fear of parting with her.

Miss Sukey Jennett said, that Rozella's laughing at her, and using her with contempt, she thought was insupportable, for who could bear the contempt of a friend?

Many and various were the remarks made by Miss Jenny's hearers on the story she had read to them. But now they were so confirmed in goodness, and every one was so settled in her affection for her companions, that, instead of being angry at any opposition that was made to their judgments, every one spoke her opinion with the utmost mildness.

Miss Jenny sat some time silent to hear their conversation on her fairy tale. But her seeing them so much altered in their manner of talking to each other, since the time they made their little remarks on her story of the giants, filled her whole mind with the most sincere pleasure; and with a smile peculiar to herself, and which diffused a cheerfulness to all around her, she told her companions the joy their present behaviour had inspired her with; but saying that it was as late as their governess chose they should stay out, she rose, and walked towards the house, whither she was cheerfully followed by the whole company.

Mrs. Teachum after supper, again, in a familiar manner, talked to them on the subject of the fairy tale, and encouraged them, as much as possible, to answer her freely in whatever she asked them; and at last said, 'My good children, I am very much pleased when you are innocently amused; and yet I would have you consider seriously enough of what you read, to draw such morals from your books, as may influence your future practice; and as to fairy tales in general, remember, that the fairies, as I told Miss Jenny before of giants and magic, are only introduced by the writers of those tales, by way of amusement to the reader. For if the story is well written, the common course of things would produce the same incidents, without the help of fairies.

'As for example, in this of the Princess Hebe, you see the queen her mother was not admitted to know the fairy's history, till she could calm her mind enough to hearken to reason; which only means, that whilst we give way to the raging of our passions, nothing useful can ever sink into our minds. For by the fairy Sybella's story you find, that by our own faults we may turn the greatest advantages into our own misery, as Sybella's mother did her beauty, by making use of the influence it gave her over her husband, to tease him into the ruin of his child; and as also Brunetta did, by depending on her father's gift, to enable her to complete her desires, and therefore never endeavouring to conquer them.

'You may observe also on the other side, that no accident had any power to hurt Sybella, because she followed the paths of virtue, and kept her mind free from restless passions.

'You see happiness in the good Sybella's peaceful grove, and misery in the wicked Brunetta's gaudy castle. The queen desiring the fairy to endow her child with true wisdom, was the cause that the Princess Hebe had it in her power to be happy. But take notice, that when she swerved from her duty, all her knowledge was of no use, but only rendered her more miserable, by letting her see her own folly in the stronger light. Rozella first tempted the princess to disobedience, by moving her tenderness, and alarming her friendship, in fearing to part with her; and then by persuading her to set up her own wisdom, in opposition to her mother's commands, rather than be laughed at, and despised by her friends. You are therefore to observe, that if you would steadily persevere in virtue, you must have resolution enough to stand the sneers of those who would allure you to vice; for it is the constant practice of the vicious, to endeavour to allure others to follow their example, by an affected contempt and ridicule of virtue.

'By the Princess Hebe's being drawn at last beyond the prescribed bounds, by the cries and entreaties of that insidious girl, you are to learn, that whatever appearance of virtue any action may be attended with, yet if it makes you go contrary to the commands of those who know better what is for your good, than you do your selves, and who can see farther into the consequences of actions than can your tender years, it will certainly lead you into error and misfortune; and you find, as soon as the princess had once overleaped the bounds, another plausible excuse arose to carry her on; and by a false fear of incurring her mother's displeasure, she really deserved that displeasure, and was soon reduced into the power of her enemy.

'The princess, you see, could have no happiness till she returned again to her obedience, and had confessed her fault. And though in this story all this is brought about by fairies, yet the moral of it is, that whenever we give way to our passions, and act contrary to our duty, we must be miserable.

'But let me once more observe to you, that these fairies are only intended to amuse you; for remember that the misery which attended the Princess Hebe, on her disobedience, was the natural consequence of that disobedience, as well as the natural consequence of her amendment and return to her duty, was content and happiness for the rest of her life.'

Here good Mrs. Teachum ceased, and Miss Jenny, in the name of the company, thanked her for her kind instructions, and promised that they would endeavour, to the utmost of their power, to imprint them on their memory for the rest of their lives.

SUNDAY. THE SEVENTH DAY.

This morning our little society rose very early, and were all dressed with neatness and elegance, in order to go to church. Mrs. Teachum put Miss Polly Suckling before her, and the rest followed, two and two, with perfect regularity.

Mrs. Teachum expressed great approbation, that her scholars, at this solemn place, showed no sort of childishness, notwithstanding their tender age; but behaved with decency and devotion suitable to the occasion.

They went again in the same order, and behaved again in the same manner, in the afternoon; and when they returned from church, two young ladies, Lady Caroline and Lady Fanny Delun, who had formerly known Miss Jenny Peace, and who were at present in that neighbourhood with their uncle, came to make her a visit.

Lady Caroline was fourteen years of age, tall and genteel in her person, of a fair complexion, and a regular set of features so that, upon the whole, she was generally complimented with being very handsome.

Lady Fanny, who was one year younger than her sister, was rather little of her age, of a brown complexion, her features irregular; and, in short, she had not the least real pretensions to beauty.

It was but lately that their father was, by the death of his eldest brother, become Earl of Delun; so that their titles were new, and they had not been long used to your ladyship.

Miss Jenny Peace received them as her old acquaintance: however, she paid them the deference due to their quality, and, at the same time, took care not to behave as if she imagined they thought of anything else.

As it was her chief delight to communicate her pleasures to others, she introduced her new-made friends to her old acquaintance, and expected to have spent a very agreeable afternoon. But to describe the behaviour of these two young ladies is very difficult. Lady Caroline, who was dressed in a pink robe, embroidered thick with gold, and adorned with very fine jewels, and the finest Mechlin lace, addressed most of her discourse to her sister, that she might have the pleasure every minute of uttering 'Your ladyship,' in order to show what she herself expected. And as she spoke, her fingers were in perpetual motion, either adjusting her tucker, placing her plaits of her robe, or fiddling with a diamond cross, that hung down on her bosom, her eyes accompanying her fingers as they moved, and then suddenly being snatched off, that she might not be observed to think of her own dress; yet was it plain, that her thoughts were employed on only that and her titles. Miss Jenny Peace, although she would have made it her choice always to have been in company who did not deserve ridicule, yet had she humour enough to treat affectation as it deserved. And she addressed herself to Lady Caroline with so many ladyships, and such praises of her fine clothes, as she hoped would have made her ashamed; but Lady Caroline was too full of her own vanity, to see her design, and only exposed herself ten times the more, till she really got the better of Miss Jenny, who blushed for her, since she was incapable of blushing for herself.

Lady Fanny's dress was plain and neat only, nor did she mention anything about it; and it was very visible her thoughts were otherwise employed, neither did she seem to take any delight in the words 'Your ladyship': but she tossed and threw her person about into so many ridiculous postures, and as there happened unfortunately to be no looking-glass in the room where they sat, she turned and rolled her eyes so many different ways, in endeavouring to view as much of herself as possible, that it was very plain to the whole company she thought herself a beauty, and admired herself for being so.

Our little society, whose hearts were so open to each other, that they had not a thought they endeavoured to conceal, were so filled with contempt at Lady Caroline and Lady Fanny's behaviour, and yet so strictly obliged, by good manners, not to show that contempt, that the reserve they were forced to put on, laid them under so great a restraint, that they knew not which way to turn themselves, or how to utter one word; and great was their joy when Lady Caroline, as the eldest, led the way, and with a swimming curtsey, her head turned half round on one shoulder, and a disdainful eye, took her leave, repeating two or three times the word 'misses,' to put them in mind, that she was a lady. She was followed by her sister Lady Fanny, who made a slow distinct curtsey to every one in the room, that she might be the longer under observation. And then taking Miss Jenny by the hand, said, 'Indeed, Miss, you are very pretty,' in order to put them in mind of her own beauty.

Our little society, as soon as they were released, retired to their arbour, where, for some time, they could talk of nothing but this visit. Miss Jenny Peace remarked how many shapes vanity would turn itself into, and desired them to observe, how ridiculously Lady Caroline Delun turned her whole thoughts on her dress, and condition of life; and how absurd it was in Lady Fanny, who was a very plain girl, to set up for a beauty, and to behave in a manner which would render her contemptible, even if she had that beauty her own vanity made her imagine herself possessed of.

Miss Nanny Spruce said, 'She was greatly rejoiced that she had seen her folly; for she could very well remember when she had the same vanity of dress and superiority of station with Lady Caroline, though she had not, indeed, a title to support it; and in what manner, she said, she would tell them in the story of her life.

THE DESCRIPTION OF MISS NANNY SPRUCE.

Miss Nanny Spruce was just nine years old, and was the very reverse of Patty Lockit, in all things; for she had little limbs, little features, and such a compactness in her form, that she was often called the little fairy. She had the misfortune to be lame in one of her hips; but by good management, and a briskness and alacrity in carrying herself, it was a very small blemish to her, and looked more like an idle childish gait, than any real defect.

THE LIFE OF MISS NANNY SPRUCE.

'My delight,' said Miss Nanny Spruce, 'ever since I can remember, has been in dress and finery; for whenever I did as I was bid, I was promised fine coats, ribbons, and laced caps; and when I was stubborn and naughty, then my fine things were all to be locked up, and I was to wear only an old stuff coat; so that I thought the only reward I could have was to be dressed fine and the only punishment was to be plainly dressed. By this means I delighted so much in fine clothes, that I never thought of anything but when I should have something new to adorn myself in; and I have sat whole days considering what should be my next new coat; for I had always my choice given me of the colour.

'We lived in a country parish, my papa being the only gentleman, so that all the little girls in the parish used to take it as a great honour to play with me. And I used to delight to show them my fine things, and to see that they could not come at any but very plain coats. However, as they did not pretend to have anything equal with me, I was kind enough to them. As to those girls whose parents were so very poor that they went in rags, I did not suffer them to come near me.

'Whilst I was at home, I spent my time very pleasantly, as no one pretended to be my equal; but as soon as I came to school, where other misses were as fine as myself, and some finer, I grew very miserable. Every new coat, every silver ribbon, that any of my schoolfellows wore, made me unhappy. Your scarlet damask, Miss Betty Ford, cost me a week's pain; and I lay awake, and sighed and wept all night, because I did not dare to spoil it. I had several plots in my head, to have dirtied it, or cut it, so as to have made it unfit to wear; by some accident my plots were prevented; and then I was so uneasy, I could not tell what to do with myself; and so afraid, lest any body should suspect me of such a thing, that I could not sleep in peace, for fear I should dream of it, and in my sleep discover it to my bedfellow. I would not go through the same dreads and terrors again for the world. But I am very happy now, in having no thoughts but what my companions may know; for since that quarrel, and Miss Jenny Peace was so good as to show me what I'm sure I never thought of before, that is, that the road to happiness is by conquering such foolish vanities, and the only way to be pleased is to endeavour to please others, I have never known what it was to be uneasy.'

As soon as Miss Nanny had finished speaking, Miss Betty Ford said, that she heartily forgave her all her former designs upon her scarlet coat; but, added she, Lady Fanny Delun put me no less in mind of my former life, than Lady Caroline did you of yours; and if Miss Jenny pleases, I will now relate it.

THE DESCRIPTION OF MISS BETTY FORD.

Miss Betty Ford was of the same age with Miss Nanny Spruce, and much of the same height, and might be called the plainest girl in the school; for she had nothing pleasing either in her person or face, except an exceeding fair skin, and tolerable good black eyes; but her face was ill-shaped and broad, her hair very red, and all the summer she was generally very full of freckles; and she had also a small hesitation in her speech. But without preamble, she began her life as follows.

THE LIFE OF MISS BETTY FORD.

'My life,' said Miss Betty Ford, 'has hitherto passed very like that of Miss Nanny Spruce, only with this difference, that as all her thoughts were fixed on finery, my head ran on nothing but beauty. I had an elder sister, who was, I must own, a great deal handsomer than me; and yet, in my own mind, at that time, I did not think so, though I was always told it was not for me to pretend to the same things with pretty Miss Kitty (which was the name of my sister); and in all respects she was taken so much more notice of than I was, that I perfectly hated her, and could not help wishing that, by some accident, her beauty might be spoiled: whenever any visitors came to the house, their praises of her gave me the greatest vexation; and as I had made myself believe I was a very great beauty, I thought that it was prejudice and ill-nature in all around me, not to view me in that light. My sister Kitty was very good natured; and though she was thus cried up for her beauty, and indulged most on that account, yet she never insulted me, but did all in her power to oblige me. But I could not love her, and sometimes would raise lies against her, which did not signify, for she could always justify herself. I could not give any reason for hating her, but her beauty, for she was very good; but the better she was, I thought the worse I appeared. I could not bear her praises without teasing and vexing myself. At last, little Kitty died of a fever, to my great joy, though, as everybody cried for her, I cried too for company, and because I would not be thought ill-natured.

'After Kitty's death, I lived tolerably easy, till I came to school. Then the same desire of beauty returned, and I hated all the misses who were handsomer than myself, as much as I had before hated my sister, and always took every opportunity of quarrelling with them, till I found my own peace was concerned, in getting the better of this disposition; and that, if I would have any content, I must not repine at my not being so handsome as others.'

When Miss Betty Ford ceased, Miss Jenny said, 'Indeed, my dear, it is well you had not at that time the power of the eagle in the fable; for your poor sister might then, like the peacock, have said in a soft voice, "You are, indeed, a great beauty; but it lies in your beak and your talons, which make it death to me to dispute it."'

Miss Betty Ford rejoiced, that her power did not extend to enable her to do mischief, before she had seen her folly. And now this little society, in good humour and cheerfulness, attended their kind governess's summons to supper; and then, after the evening prayers, they retired to their peaceful slumbers.

MONDAY. THE EIGHTH DAY.

Early in the morning, after the public prayers which Mrs. Teachum read every day, our little company took a walk in the garden whilst the breakfast was preparing.

The fine weather, the prospects round them, all conspired to increase their pleasure. They looked at one another with delight; their minds were innocent and satisfied; and therefore every outward object was pleasing in their sight.

Miss Jenny Peace said, she was sure they were happier than any other society of children whatever, except where the same harmony and love were preserved, as were kept up in their minds: 'For (continued she) I think now, my dear companions, I can answer for you all, that no mischievous, no malicious plots disturb the tranquility of your thoughts; plots, which in the end, constantly fall on the head of those who invent them, after all the pains they cost in forming, and endeavouring to execute.'

Whilst Miss Jenny Peace was talking, Miss Dolly Friendly looked at her very earnestly. She would not interrupt her; but the moment she was silent, Miss Dolly said, 'My dear Miss Jenny, what is the matter with you? your eyes are swelled, and you look as if you had been crying. If you have any grief that you keep to yourself, you rob us of the share we have a right to demand in all that belongs to you.'

'No, indeed (answered Miss Jenny), I have nothing that grieves me; though, if I had, I should think it increased, rather than lessened, by your being grieved too; but last night, after I went upstairs, I found amongst my books the play of the Funeral, or, Grief-a-la-mode; where the faithful and tender behaviour of a good old servant, who had long lived in his lord's family, with many other passages in the play (which I cannot explain, unless you knew the whole story) made me cry, so that I could hardly stop my tears.'

'Pray, Miss Jenny, let us hear this play, that had such an effect on you,' was the general request; and Miss Jenny readily promised, when they met in their arbour, to read it to them.

They eagerly ran to their arbour as soon as school was over, and Miss Jenny performed her promise, and was greatly pleased to find such a sympathy between her companions and herself; for they were most of them affected just in the same manner, and with the same parts of the play, as had before affected her.

By the time they had wiped their eyes, and were rejoicing at the turn at the end of the play, in favour of the characters with which they were most pleased, Mrs. Teachum entered the arbour, and inquired what they had been reading. Miss Jenny immediately told her, adding, 'I hope, Madam, you will not think reading a play an improper amusement for us; for I should be very sorry to be guilty myself, or cause my companions to be guilty, of any thing that would meet with your disapprobation.' Mrs. Teachum answered, that she was not at all displeased with her having read a play, as she saw by her fear of offending, that her discretion was to be trusted to. 'Nay (continued this good woman), I like that you should know something of all kinds of writings, where neither morals nor manners are offended; for if you read plays, and consider them as you ought, you will neglect and despise what is light and useless, whilst you will imprint on your mind's every useful lesson that is to be drawn from them. I am very well acquainted with the play you have been reading; but that I may see whether you give the proper attention to what you have heard, I desire, my little girls, that one of you will give me an account of the chief incidents in the play, and tell me the story, just as you would do to one of your companions that had happened to have been absent.'

Here they all looked upon Miss Jenny Peace, as thinking her the most capable of doing what their governess required. But Mrs. Teachum, reading their thoughts in their looks, said, 'I exclude Miss Jenny in this case; for as the play was of her choosing to read to you, I doubt not but she is thoroughly enough acquainted with every part of it; and my design was to try the memory and attention of some of the others.'

They all remained silent, and seemed to wait for a more particular command, before any one would offer at the undertaking; not through any backwardness to comply with Mrs. Teachum's request, but each from a diffidence of herself to perform it.

Miss Jenny Peace then said, that she had observed a great attention in them all; and she did not doubt but every one was able to give a very good account of what they had heard. 'But, as Miss Sukey Jennet is the eldest, I believe, madam, (continued she), if you approve it, they will all be very ready to depute her as their speaker.'

Each smiled at being so relieved by Miss Jenny; and Mrs. Teachum, taking Miss Sukey Jennet by the hand, said, 'Come, my dear, throw off all fear and reserve; imagine me one of your companions, and tell me the story of the play you have been reading.'

Miss Sukey, thus encouraged by her kind governess, without any hesitation, spoke in the following manner:

'If I understand your commands, madam, by telling the story of the play, you would not have me tell you the acts and scenes as they followed one another for that I am afraid I can hardly remember, as I have heard it only once but I must describe the chief people in the play, and the plots and contrivances that are carried on amongst them.'

Mrs. Teachum nodded her head, and Miss Sukey thus proceeded:

''There is an old Lord Brumpton, who had married a young wife, that had lived with him some years, and by her deceitful and cunning ways had prevailed with him to disinherit his only son Lord Hardy (who was a very sensible good young man) and to leave him but a shilling. And this Lord Brumpton was taken in a fit, so that all the house thought he was dead, and his lady sent for an undertaker, one Mr. Sable, to bury him. But coming out of his fit, when nobody but this Mr. Sable, and an old servant, called Trusty, were by, he was prevailed upon by the good old Trusty to feign himself still dead (and the undertaker promises secrecy) in order to detect the wickedness of his wife, which old Trusty assures him is very great; and then he carries his lord where he overhears a discourse between the widow (as she thinks herself) and her maid Tattleaid; and he bears his once beloved wife rejoicing in his supposed death, and in the success of her own arts to deceive him. Then there are two young ladies, Lady Charlotte and Lady Harriet Lovely, to whom this Lord Brumpton was guardian; and he had also left them in the care of this wicked woman. And this young Lord Hardy was in love with Lady Charlotte; and Mr. Camply, a very lively young gentleman, his friend, was in love with Lady Harriet and Lady Brumpton locked the two young ladies up, and would not let them be seen by their lovers. But there at last they contrived, by the help of old Trusty, who had their real guardian's consent for it, both to get away; and Lady Harriet married Mr. Camply directly; but Lady Charlotte did not get away so soon, and so was not married till the end of the play. This Mr. Camply was a very generous man, and was newly come to a large fortune; and in the beginning of the play he contrives, in a very genteel manner, to give his friend Lord Hardy, who very much wanted it, three hundred pounds; but he takes care to let us know, that my lord had formerly, when he waited his assistance, been very kind to him. And there at last, when Lady Brumpton finds out that the two young ladies are gone, she goes away in a rage to Lord Hardy's lodgings, and in an insulting manner she pays all due legacies, as she calls it, that is, she gives Lord Hardy the shilling, which, by her wicked arts, was all his father had left him; and she was insulting the young ladies, and glorying in her wickedness, when honest old Trusty came in, and brought in old Lord Brumpton, whom they imagined to be dead, and all but Lady Brumpton were greatly overjoyed to see him alive; but when he taxed her with her falsehood, she defied him, and said that she had got a deed of gift under his hand, which he could not revoke, and she WOULD enjoy his fortune in spite of him. Upon which they all looked sadly vexed, till the good old Trusty went out and came in again, and brought in a man called Cabinet, who confessed himself the husband to the pretended Lady Brumpton, and that he was married to her half a year before she was married to my Lord Brumpton; but as my lord happened to fall in love with her, they agreed to keep their marriage concealed, in order that she should marry my lord, and cheat him in the manner she had done; and the reason that Cabinet came to confess all this was, that he looked into a closet and saw my lord writing, after he thought he was dead, and, taking it for his ghost, was by that means frightened into this confession, which he first made in writing to old Trusty, and therefore could not now deny it. They were all rejoiced at this discovery, except the late pretended Lady Brumpton, who sneaked away with Cabinet her husband; and my Lord Brumpton embraced his son, and gave his consent, that he should marry Lady Charlotte; and they were all pleased and happy.'

Here Miss Sukey ceased, and Mrs. Teachum told her she was a very good girl, and had remembered a great deal of the play. 'But (said she) in time, with using yourself to this way of repeating what you have read, you will come to a better manner, and a more regular method of telling your story, which you was now so intent upon finishing, that you forgot to describe what sort of women those two young ladies were, though, as to all the rest, you have been particular enough.'

'Indeed, madam, (said Miss Sukey), I had forgot that, but Lady Charlotte was a very sensible, grave young lady, and lady Harriet was extremely gay and coquettish; but Mr. Camply tells her how much it misbecomes her to be so and she having good sense, as well as good nature, is convinced of her folly, and likes him so well for his reproof, that she consents to marry him.'

Mrs. Teachum, addressing herself to them all, told them, that this was a method she wished they would take with whatever they read; for nothing so strongly imprinted anything on the memory as such a repetition; and then turning to Miss Jenny Peace, she said, 'And now, Miss Jenny, I desire you will speak freely what you think is the chief moral to be drawn from the play you have just read.'

Miss Jenny being thus suddenly asked a question of this nature, considered some time before she gave an answer; for she was naturally very diffident of her own opinion in anything where she had not been before instructed by some one she thought wiser than herself. At last, with a modest look, and an humble voice, she said, 'Since, madam, you have commanded me to speak my sentiments freely, I think by what happened to each character in this play, the author intended to prove what my good mamma first taught me, and what you, madam, since have so strongly confirmed me in; namely, that folly, wickedness, and misery, all three, as constantly dwell together, as wisdom, virtue, and happiness do.'

"Tis very true (answered Mrs. Teachum); but this moral does not arise only from the happy turn in favour of the virtuous characters in the conclusion of the play, but is strongly inculcated, as you see all along, in the peace of mind that attends the virtuous, even in the midst of oppression and distress, while the event is yet doubtful, and apparently against them; and, on the contrary, in the confusion of mind which the vicious are tormented with, even whilst they falsely imagine themselves triumphant.'

Mrs. Teachum then taking the book out of Miss Jenny's hands, and turning to the passage, said, 'How does Lady Brumpton show us the wretched condition of her own mind, when she says,

'"How miserable 'tis to have one one hates always about one! And when one can't endure one's own reflections upon some actions, who can bear the thoughts of another upon them?"

'Then with what perturbation of mind does she proceed, to wish it was in her power to increase her wickedness, without making use enough of her understanding, to see that by that means she would but increase her own misery.

'On the other hand, what a noble figure does Lord Hardy make, when, by this wicked woman's contrivances, he thinks himself disinherited of his whole fortune, ill-treated, and neglected by a father, he never had in thought offended! He could give an opportunity to a sincere friend, who would not flatter him, to say,

'"No; you are, my lord, the extraordinary man, who, on the loss of an almost princely fortune, can be master of a temper that makes you the envy rather than pity, of your more fortunate, not more happy friends."

'This is a fine distinction between fortunate and happy; and intimates this happiness must dwell in the mind, and depends upon no outward accidents.

'Fortune, indeed, is a blessing, if properly used; which Camply shows, when by that means he can assist and relieve his worthy friend.

'With what advantage does Lady Charlotte appear over her sister, when the latter is trifling and dancing before the glass, and the former says,

'"If I am at first so silly as to be a little taken with myself, I know it is a fault, and take pains to correct it."

'And on Lady Harriet's saying, very giddily, that it was too soon for her to think at that rate, Lady Charlotte properly adds,

'"They that think it too soon to understand themselves, will very soon find it too late."

'In how ridiculous a light does Lady Harriet appear, while she is displaying all that foolish coquetry! And how different a figure does she make, when she has got the better of it?

'My Lady Brumpton, when alarmed with the least noise, breaks out into all the convulsive starts natural to conscious guilt.

'"Ha! what noise is that—that noise of fighting?—Run, I say.—Whither are you going?—What, are you mad?—Will you leave me alone?—Can't you stir?—What, you can't take your message with you!—Whatever 'tis, I suppose you are not in the plot, not you—nor that now they're breaking open my house for Charlotte—Not you.—Go see what's the matter, I say; I have nobody I can trust.—One minute I think this wench honest, and the next false.—Whither shall I turn me?"

'This is a picture of the confused, the miserable mind of a close, malicious, cruel, designing woman, as Lady Brumpton was, and as Lady Harriet very properly calls her.

'Honesty and faithfulness shine forth in all their lustre, in the good old Trusty. We follow him throughout with anxious wishes for his success, and tears of joy for his tenderness. And when he finds that he is likely to come at the whole truth, and to save his lord from being deceived and betrayed into unjustly ruining his noble son, you may remember that he makes this pious reflection:

All that is ours, is to be justly bent; And Heaven in its own time will bless th' event.

'This is the natural thought that proceeds from innocence and goodness; and surely this state of mind is happiness.

'I have only pointed out a few passages, to show you, that though it is the nature of comedy to end happily, and therefore the good characters must be successful in the last act; yet the moral lies deeper, and is to be deduced from a proof throughout this play, that the natural consequence of vice is misery within, even in the midst of an apparent triumph; and the natural consequence of goodness is a calm peace of mind, even in the midst of oppression and distress.

'I have endeavoured, my little dears, to show you, as clearly as I can, not only what moral is to be drawn from this play, but what is to be sought for in all others; and where that moral is not to be found, the writer will have it to answer for, that he has been guilty of one of the worst of evils; namely, that he has clothed vice in so beautiful a dress, that, instead of deterring, it will allure and draw into its snares the young and tender mind. And I am sorry to say, that too many of our dramatic performances are of this latter cast; which is the reason, that wise and prudent parents and governors in general discourage in very young people the reading of plays. And though by what I have said (if it makes a proper impression) I doubt not but you will all have a just abhorrence of such immoral plays, instead of being pleased with them, should they fall in your way; yet I would advise you rather to avoid them, and never to read any but such as are approved of; and recommended to you by those who have the care of your education.'

Here good Mrs. Teachum ceased, and left her little scholars to reflect on what she had been saying; when Miss Jenny Peace declared, for her part, that she could feel the truth of her governess's observations; for she had rather be the innocent Lord Hardy, though she was to have but that one shilling in the world which was so insolently offered him as his father's last legacy, than be the Lady Brumpton, even though she had possessed the fortune she so treacherously endeavoured to obtain.

'Nay (said Miss Dolly Friendly) I had rather have been old Trusty, with all the infirmities of age, following my Lord Hardy through the world, had his poverty and distress been ever so great, than have been the malicious Lady Brumpton, in the height of her beauty, surrounded by a crowd of lovers and flatterers.'

Miss Henny Fret then declared how glad she was that she had now no malice in her mind; though she could not always have said so, as she would inform them in the history of her past life.

THE DESCRIPTION OF MISS HENNY FRET.

Miss Henny Fret was turned of nine years old. She was very prettily made, and remarkably genteel. All her features were regular. She was not very fair, and looked pale. Her upper lip seemed rather shorter than it should be; for it was drawn up in such a manner, as to show her upper teeth; and though this was in some degree natural, yet it had been very much increased by her being continually on the fret for every trifling accident that offended her, or on every contradiction that was offered to her. When you came to examine her face, she had not one feature but what was pretty; yet, from that constant uneasiness which appeared in her countenance, it gave you so little pleasure to look at her, that she seldom had common justice done her, but had generally hitherto passed for a little insignificant plain girl, though her very face was so altered since she was grown good natured, and had got the better of that foolish fretfulness she used to be possessed of, that she appeared from her good-humoured smiles quite a different person; and, with a mild aspect, thus began her story:

THE LIFE OF MISS HENNY FRET.

'I had one brother,' said Miss Henny, 'as well as Miss Jenny Peace; but my manner of living with him was quite the reverse to that in which she lived with her brother. All my praise or blame was to arise from my being better or worse than my brother. If I was guilty of any fault, it was immediately said, "Oh! fie, miss! Master George (that was my brother's name) would not be guilty of such a thing for the world." If he was carried abroad, and I stayed at home, then I was bemoaned over, that poor Miss Henny was left at home, and her brother carried abroad. And then I was told, that I should go abroad one of these days, and my brother be left at home so that whenever I went abroad, my greatest joy was, that he was left at home; and I was pleased to see him come out to the coach-door with a melancholy air that he could not go too. If my brother happened to have any fruit given him, and was in a peevish humour, and would not give me as much as I desired, the servant that attended me was sure to bid me take care, when I had anything he waited, not to give him any. So that I thought, if I did not endeavour to be revenged of him, I should show a want of spirit, which was of all things what I dreaded most. I had a better memory than my brother, and whenever I learnt anything, my comfort was to laugh at him because he could not learn so fast; by which means I got a good deal of learning, but never minded what I learnt, nor took any pains to keep it; so that what I was eager to learn one day, to show George how much I knew more than he, I forgot the next. And so I went on learning, and forgetting as fast as I learnt; and all the pains I took served only to show that I COULD learn.

'I was so great a favourite, that I was never denied any thing I asked for; but I was very unhappy for the same reason that Miss Dolly Friendly's sister was so; and I have often sat down and cried, because I did not know what I would have, till at last I own I grew so peevish and humoursome, that I was always on the fret, and harboured in my mind a kind of malice that made me fancy whatever my brother got, I lost; and in this unhappy condition I lived, till I came to school, and here I found that other misses wanted to have their humours as well as myself. This I could not bear, because I had been used to have my own will, and never to trouble myself about what others felt. For whenever I beat or abused my brother, his pain did not make me cry; but I believe it was thinking wrong made me guilty of these faults; for I don't find I am ill-natured; for now I have been taught to consider that my companions can feel as well as myself, I am sorry for their pain, and glad when they are pleased, and would be glad to do anything to oblige them.'

Here Miss Henny ceased, and Miss Jenny Peace then told her how glad she was to hear that she had subdued all malice in her mind, adding, 'These weeds, my dear, unless early plucked up, are (as I have heard our good governess observe upon a like occasion) very apt to take such deep root, as to choke every good seed around them; and then who can tell whether, with the same opportunities, they might not become Lady Brumptons before the end of their lives?'

Little Polly Suckling remembered that all the company had told the story of their past lives, except herself; and she thought she would not be left out; but yet she had a mind to be asked to tell it, hoping that her companions thought her of consequence enough not to leave her out of any scheme; therefore, addressing herself to Miss Jenny, she said she thought it was very pleasant to hear anybody tell the history of their own lives. Miss Jenny saw her meaning, and answered, 'So it is, my little dear; and now, if you please, you shall oblige us with relating the history of yours.' Polly smiled at this request, and said she was ready to comply.

THE DESCRIPTION OF MISS POLLY SUCKLING.

Miss Polly Suckling was just turned of eight years old, but so short of her age, that few people took her to be above five. It was not a dwarfish shortness; for she had the most exact proportioned limbs in the world, very small bones, and was as fat as a little cherub. She was extremely fair, and her hair quite flaxen. Her eyes a perfect blue, her mouth small, and her lips quite plump and red. She had the freshness of a milkmaid; and when she smiled and laughed, she seemed to show an hundred agreeable dimples. She was, in short, the very picture of health and good-humour, and was the plaything and general favorite of the whole school.

THE LIFE OF MISS POLLY SUCKLING.

'Now,' said little Polly, 'I will tell you all my whole history. I hardly remember anything before I came to school, for I was but five years old when I was brought hither.

'All I know is, that I don't love quarrelling, for I like better to live in peace and quietness. But I have been always less than any of my companions, ever since I have been here; and so I only followed the example of the rest; and as I found they contended about everything, I did so too. Besides, I have been always in fear that my schoolfellows wanted to impose on me, because I was little; and so I used to engage in every quarrel, rather than be left out, as if I was too little to give any assistance; but, indeed, I am very glad now we all agree, because I always came by the worst of it. And, besides, it is a great pleasure to me to be loved, and every Miss is kind and good to me, and ready to assist me whenever I ask them. And this is all I know of my whole life.'

When little Polly ceased, she was kissed and applauded by the whole company, for the agreeable simplicity of her little history.

And thus ended the eighth day's amusement.

TUESDAY. THE NINTH DAY.

Miss Jenny rose early in the morning, and, having collected the lives of her companions (which she had wrote down each day, as they related them) she carried them, after morning school, according to her promise, to her governess.

Mrs. Teachum, when she had perused them, was much pleased; and said that she perceived, by the manner in which her scholars had related their lives, how much they were in earnest in their design of amendment. 'For (continued she) they have all confessed their faults without reserve; and the untowardly bent of their minds, which so strongly appeared before the quarrel, has not broke out in these their little histories; but, on the contrary, they all seem, according to their capacities, to have endeavoured at imitating your style, in the account you gave of your own life. I would have you continue to employ your leisure hours in the manner you have lately done, only setting apart a proper time for exercise; and today I will dispense with your attendance in the school-room and indulge you this afternoon in another walk, either to the dairy house, or to the cherry-garden, whichever you all agree on. But as I shall not go with you myself, and shall only find a servant to take care of you, I hope to hear from you, Miss Jenny, so good an account of the behaviour of your little friends and companions, that I shall have no cause to repent my indulgence.'

Miss Jenny Peace respectfully took leave of her governess, and hastened to the arbour, where her little friends were met, in expectation of her coming. She told them how well pleased their governess was with them all, for the ingenuous confession of their faults in their past lives; and she then declared Mrs. Teachum's kind permission to them to take another walk that afternoon.

As no one had at present any story to read or relate, they employed their time till dinner, some in walking and running about the garden; others in looking after and tending some plant or flower, that they had taken particularly under their care, which Mrs. Teachum both permitted and encouraged them in, whilst Miss Jenny Peace, Miss Sukey Jennett, and Miss Dolly Friendly, remained in the arbour, the two latter asking a thousand questions of the former, both concerning all the instructions she had ever learned from her mamma, and by what means they should best be able to preserve that friendship and happiness, which had of late subsisted amongst them; saying, how pleased their friends and relations would be, to see such a change in their temper and behaviour, and how much they should be beloved by every one.

When they met at dinner, Mrs. Teachum asked them, whether they had determined upon the choice she had given them in their afternoon's walk; and they were all desirous of going to the dairy house; for little Polly said, she longed to see the good-humoured old woman again, and, indeed, she would not now say anything to her of her shaking head, or her grey hair. Mrs. Teachum was pleased, that little Polly so gratefully remembered the old woman, who had been so kind to her; and readily consented to their choice, and approved of their determination.

Being soon equipped for their walk, they set out, attended by two maidservants; and as soon as they arrived, the good old woman expressed the highest joy on seeing them, and told little Polly, that she should have plenty of cream and strawberries, for her daughter had been that day in the wood, and had brought home three baskets of very fine ones. Mrs. Nelly, her daughter, said very crossly, that she supposed there would be fine work amongst them, now their governess was not with them; but 'twas her mother's way, to let all children be as rude as they pleased. Miss Sukey Jennett, with some indignation in her look, was going to answer her; but Miss Jenny Peace, fearing she would say something less mild than she wished, gave her a nod; and, turning to the young woman, with great modesty and temper, thus said: 'You shall see, Mrs. Nelly, that our good governess's instructions are of more force with us, than to lose all their effect when we are out of her presence; and I hope you will have no cause, when we go away, to complain of the ill behaviour of any of us.'

The good old woman declared she never saw such sweet-tempered children in all her life; and after they had eat their strawberries and cream, and were loaded with pinks and roses by the good woman's bounty (for they did not gather one without her permission), they took their leave with the utmost civility, and Miss Jenny handsomely rewarded the old woman for her good cheer. Mrs. Nelly herself was so pleased with their regular and inoffensive behaviour, that she could not help telling Miss Jenny, that she, and all her companions, had, indeed, behaved as well as if their governess had been with them: on which Miss Jenny (as they were walking home) observed to Miss Sukey Jennett (whom she had prevented from making any reply to Mrs. Nelly's speech) how much better it was to gain another's good will by our own endeavours to be obliging, than to provoke them to be more cross, by our angry answers and reproaches.

When this little company, employed in pleasing talk and lively observations, were come within about a mile of Mrs. Teachum's house, and within view of a nobleman's fine seat, Miss Jenny said, that the next time their governess permitted them to walk out, she would ask her leave, that they might go and see that fine house; for some time ago she had told them, that they should go thither when the family were absent. Mrs. Wilson, the housekeeper, who by chance was walking that way, and heard what Miss Jenny said, came up to them, and told Miss Jenny that her lord and lady were now both absent, having set out, one for London, and the other for another fine seat, forty miles off, that very morning; and as she knew them to be Mrs. Teachum's well-regulated family, they should be welcome to see the house and gardens now, if they liked it. Miss Jenny thanked her, and said, as it was near two hours sooner than their governess expected them home, she would accept of her kind offer. The housekeeper led them through an avenue of tall elm-trees into this magnificent house, in which were many spacious apartments, furnished with the utmost grandeur and elegance. Some of the rooms were adorned with fine pictures, others were hung with tapestry almost as lively as those paintings, and most of the apartments above stairs were furnished with the finest sorts of needle-work. Our little company were struck into a sort of silent wonder and admiration at the splendid appearance of everything around them; nor could they find words to express the various reflections that passed in their minds, on seeing such a variety of dazzling gaudy things: but when they came to the needlework, Miss Jenny could not help smiling, to see how every one seemed most fixed in attention upon that sort of work, which she herself was employed in, and she saw in every face a secret wish, that their own piece of work might be finished with equal neatness and perfection. The housekeeper was greatly pleased to see them so much delighted, and answered all their questions concerning the stories that were represented in the pictures and tapestry as fully as the time would permit; but Miss Jenny, being fearful of exceeding the hour in which they would be expected home, told them they must not now stay any longer, but if their governess would give them leave, and it would not be troublesome to Mrs. Wilson, they would come another time. She answered, that it was so far from being troublesome, that she never had more pleasure in her life, than to see so many well-behaved young ladies, who all seemed not only pleased with what they saw, but doubly delighted, and happy, in seeing each other so; and for her part, she could wish they were to stay with her all their lives; and, in short, they should not go till they had been in her room, and eat some sweetmeats of her own making. The good woman seemed to take so much delight in giving them any pleasure, that Miss Jenny could not refuse accepting her offer; and, when they were all in her room, Polly Suckling said, 'Well, this is a most charming house; I wish we could all live here for ever. How happy must the lord and lady of this fine place be!'

'Indeed, my little Polly,' said Miss Jenny, 'you may be very much mistaken; for you know our good governess has taught us, that there is no happiness but in the content of our own minds; and perhaps we may have more pleasure in viewing these fine things, than the owners have in the possession of them.'

'It is very true,' said the housekeeper, 'for my lord and lady have no delight in all this magnificence; for, by being so accustomed to it, they walk through all these apartments, and never so much as observe or amuse themselves with the work, the pictures, or anything else, or if they observe them at all, it is rather with a look that denotes a sort of weariness, at seeing the same things continually before them, than with any kind of pleasure.' And then, with a deep sigh, she added, 'You are, indeed, young lady, perfectly in the right, when you say grandeur and happiness do not always go together.' But turning off the discourse, Mrs. Wilson forced them to take as many dried sweetmeats as they could carry away with them, and insisted upon their promise (with Mrs. Teachum's consent) that they should come another time to see the gardens. They then took their leave with many thanks, and the greatest civility; and discoursed all the way home, on the fine things they had seen. Miss Betty Ford said, that the fine gilding, and so many glittering looking-glasses, made her think herself in Barbarico's great hall, where he kept all his treasure.

'No,' says Miss Nancy Spruce, 'it was not half so much like that, as it was like Brunetta's fine castle; and I could not help thinking myself the Princess Hebe, and how much I should have been pleased with such a fine place at first, just as she was.'

'Indeed,' says Miss Betty Ford, 'you are in the right of it, Miss Nanny; for 'twas much more like the description of Brunetta's castle, than what I said myself.'

Miss Jenny was pleased to hear Miss Betty so ready to own herself mistaken; and said to Miss Nanny Spruce, 'I am glad, my dear, to find that you so well remember what you read; for it is by recalling frequently into our memories the things we have read, that they are likely to be of any service to us.'

Being now come home, they entered into the presence of their governess with that pleasure, and proper confidence, which ever attends innocence and goodness; and Mrs. Teachum received them with a pleasing smile.

Miss Jenny gave her governess a faithful account of all that had passed, with the agreeable entertainment they had accidentally met with, of seeing Lord X——'s fine house, and the great civility of Mrs. Wilson, 'Which I hope, madam,' said Miss Jenny, 'I did not do wrong in accepting.' 'You did very properly, my dear,' said Mrs. Teachum, 'for when any person is willing to oblige you, without any inconvenience to themselves, it is always right to accept their offer, as you thereby gratify them, by putting it in their power to give you pleasure.'

Miss Jenny then with great cheerfulness and freedom, told her governess all that had paled in conversation, both in their walk to the dairy house, and at Lord X—'s, what little Polly had said in the housekeeper's room, as also Mrs. Wilson's answer; and said, by Mrs. Wilson's downcast look, she was afraid that poor Lord X—— and his lady were not so happy as might be wished. 'But,' continued she, 'I did not ask Mrs. Wilson any questions, because you have taught me, madam, carefully to avoid the least appearance of impertinent curiosity.'

'You was very right, my dear,' said Mrs. Teachum, 'in asking no farther questions; nor would she, I dare say, as she is a prudent woman, have gratified you if you had; for though the unhappy story is too well known all over the country, yet it would have been very unbecoming in one of the family to have published it.' Mrs. Teachum saw in her little scholars' eyes, a secret wish of knowing what this story was; and, after a short pause, she said, 'Since I find you disposed, my good girls, to make the proper use of what you hear, I will indulge your curiosity.

'Lord X—— and his lady have been married seven years; Lord X—— is the wretchedest creature breathing, because he has no children, and therefore no heir to his title and large estate. He was naturally of a haughty impetuous temper, and impatient of any the least disappointment; and this disposition not being subdued in his youth, has led him into

58

all sort of excesses. His lady is not much better tempered than himself, and valuing herself highly upon her beauty, and the large fortune she brought him, greatly resents his sometimes insolent, and always neglectful usage of her. They have hitherto lived on in the most jarring, disputing manner, and took no care to conceal their quarrels from the world; but at last they have agreed to part by consent, and the different journeys they this morning took, I suppose, was with an intent of final separation.

'That grandeur and happiness do not always go together (as Mrs. Wilson observed to you) is seen by this story, which I was the more willing to tell you, as it was a proper introduction to a fable I have been collecting together from others, for your use. You know that all my endeavours to make you good, are only intended to make you happy; and if you thoroughly reflect upon the truth of this maxim, which I so often endeavour to inculcate, you will doubtless reap no small advantage from it.'

Here Mrs. Teachum ceased speaking, and, giving Miss Jenny Peace a paper, she bid her read it aloud; which she did, and it contained the following fable:

THE ASSEMBLY OF THE BIRDS. A FABLE.

In ancient days, there was a great contention amongst the birds, which, from his own perfections, and peculiar advantages, had the strongest title to happiness; and at last they agreed to refer the decision of the debate to the eagle.

A day was appointed for their meeting; the eagle took his seat, and the birds all attended to give in their several pleas.

First spoke the parrot. Her voice so dearly resembling human speech, and which enabled her to converse with such a superior race, she doubted not (she said) would have its just weight with the eagle, and engage him to grant a decree in her favour; and to this plea she also added, that she dwelt in a fine cage adorned with gold, and was fed every day by the hands a fair lady.

'And pray, Mrs. Poll,' said the eagle, 'how comes it, since you fare so sumptuously, that you are so lean and meagre, and seem scarcely able to exert that voice you thus make your boast of?' 'Alas!' replied the parrot, 'poor Poll's lady has kept her bed almost this week; the servants have all forgot to feed me; and I am almost starved.' 'Pray observe,' said the eagle, 'the folly of such pride! Had you been able to have conversed only with your own kind, you would have fared in common with them; but it is to this vaunted imitation of the human voice, that you owe your confinement, and consequently (though living in a golden cage) your dependence upon the will and memory of others, even for common necessary food.'

Thus reproved, the parrot, with shame, hastily retired from the assembly.

Next stood forth the daw, and, having tricked himself in all the gay feathers he could muster together, on the credit of these borrowed ornaments, pleaded his beauty, as a title to the preference in dispute. Immediately the birds agreed to divest the silly counterfeit of all his borrowed plumes; and, more abashed than the parrot, he secretly slunk away.

The peacock, proud of native beauty, now flew into the midst of the assembly. He displayed before the sun his gorgeous tail. 'Observe (said he) how the vivid blue of the sapphire glitters in my neck; and when thus I spread my tail, a gemmy brightness strikes the eye from a plumage varied with a thousand glowing colours.' At this moment, a nightingale began to chant forth his melodious lay; at which the peacock, dropping his expanded tail, cried out, 'Ah what avails my silent unmeaning beauty, when I am so far excelled in voice by such a little russet-feathered wretch as that!' And, by retiring, he gave up all claim to the contended-for preference.

The nightingale was so delighted with having got the better of the peacock, that he exerted his little voice, and was so lost in the conceit of his own melody, that he did not observe a hawk, who flew upon him, and carried him off in his claws.

The eagle then declared, 'That as the peacock's envy had taken away all his claim, so no less had the nightingale's self-conceit frustrated all his pretensions; for those who are so wrapped up in their own perfections, as to mind nothing but themselves, are forever liable to all sorts of accidents.' And, besides, it was plain, by the exultation the nightingale expressed on his imagined glory over the peacock, that he would have been equally dejected on any preference given to another.

And now the owl, with an affected gravity, and whooting voice, pleaded his well-known wisdom; and said, 'He doubted not but the preference would be granted to him without contest, by all the whole assembly for what was so likely to produce happiness as wisdom?'

The eagle declared, 'That, if his title to wisdom could be proved, the justice of his claim should be allowed; and then asked him, how he could convince them of the truth of what he had advanced?' The owl answered, 'That he would willingly appeal to the whole assembly for their decision in this point; for he was positive nobody could deny his great superiority as to wisdom.' Being separately asked, they most of them declared, that they knew no one reason, either from his words or actions, to pronounce him a wise bird; though it was true, that by an affected solemnity in his looks, and by frequent declarations of his own, that he was very wife, he had made some very silly birds give him that character; but, since they were called upon to declare their opinions, they must say, that he was ever the object of contempt to all those birds who had any title to common understanding. The eagle then said, 'He could by no means admit a plea, which as plainly appeared to be counterfeit, as were the jay's borrowed feathers.' The owl, thus disappointed, flew away, and has ever since shunned the light of the sun, and has never appeared in the daytime, but to be scorned and wondered at.

It would be endless to repeat all the several pleas brought by the birds, each desiring to prove, that happiness ought to be his own peculiar lot. But the eagle observing that the arguments made use of to prove their point were chiefly drawn from the disadvantages of others, rather than from any advantage of their own, told them, 'There was too much envy and malice amongst them, for him to pronounce any of them deserving or capable of being happy; but I wonder,' says he, 'why the dove alone is absent from this meeting?' 'I know of one in her nest hard by,' answered the redbreast, 'shall I go and call her?' 'No,' says the eagle, 'since she did not obey our general summons, 'tis plain she had no ambition for a public preference; but I will take two or three chosen friends, and we will go softly to her nest, and see in what manner she is employing herself; for from our own observations upon the actions of any one, we are more likely to form a judgment of them, than by any boasts they can make.'

The eagle was obeyed, and, accompanied only by the linnet, the lark, the lapwing, and the redbreast for his guide, he stole gently to the place where the dove was found hovering over her nest, waiting the return of her absent mate; and, thinking herself quite unobserved,

[*] *While o'er her callow brood she hung,   She fondly thus address'd her young: 'Ye tender objects of my care,   Peace! peace! ye little helpless pair.   Anon! he comes, your gentle sire, And brings you all your hearts require;   For us, his infants and his bride,   For us, with only love to guide,   Our lord assumes an eagle's speed,   And, like a lion, dares to bleed: Nor yet by wintry skies confin'd,   He mounts upon the rudest wind,   From danger tears the vital spoil,   And with affection sweetens toil.   Ah! cease, too vent'rous, cease to dare;   In thine, our dearer safety spare. From him, ye cruel falcons stray;   And turn, ye fowlers, far away,   —All-giving Pow'r, great source of life,   Oh! hear the parent, hear the wife: That life thou lendest from above,   Though little, make it large in love.   Oh! bid my feeling heart expand   To ev'ry claim on ev'ry hand,   To those, from whom my days I drew,   To these in whom those days renew,   To all my kin, however wide,   In cordial warmth as blood allied.   To friends in steely fetters twin'd   And to the cruel not unkind;   But chief the lord of my desire,   My life, myself, my soul, my sire,   Friends, children, all that wish can claim, Chaste passion clasp, and rapture name.   Oh! spare him, spare him, gracious Pow'r: Oh! give him to my latest hour,   Let me my length of life employ,   To give my sole enjoyment joy.   His love let mutual love excite;   Turn all my cares to his delight,   And ev'ry needless blessing spare,   Wherein my darling wants a share.   —Let one unruffled calm delight   The loving and belov'd unite;   One pure desire our bosoms warm;   One will direct, one wish inform;   Through life one mutual aid sustain; In death one peaceful grave contain.'   While, swelling with the darling theme,   Her accents pour'd an endless stream.   The well-known wings a sound impart   That reach'd her ear, and touch'd her heart. Quick dropp'd the music of her tongue,   And forth, with eager joy, she sprung.   As swift her ent'ring*

consort flew,   And plum'd, and kindled at the view.   Their wings, their souls, embracing, meet,   Their hearts with answ'ring measure beat,   Half lost in sacred sweets, and bless'd   With raptures felt, but ne'er express'd.   Strait to her humble roof she led   The partner of her spotless bed;   Her young, a flutt'ring pair, arise,   Their welcome sparkling in their eyes,   Transported, to their sire they bound,   And hang, with speechless action, round.   In pleasure wrapt, the parents stand,   And see their little wings expand;   The sire his life sustaining prize   To each expecting bill applies;   There fondly pours the wheaten spoil,   With transport giv'n, though won with toil;   While, all collected at the sight,   And silent through supreme delight,   The fair high heav'n of bliss beguiles,   And on her lord and infants smiles.

[*] These verses are a quotation from that tender fable of   the Sparrow and the Dove, in the 'Fables for the Female   Sex.'

The eagle now, without any hesitation, pronounced the dove to be deservedly the happiest of the feathered kind; and however unwilling the rest of the birds were to assent to the judgment given, yet could they not dispute the justice of the decree.

Here Miss Jenny ceased reading, and all the little company expressed by their looks, that they were overjoyed at the eagle's determination; for they had all in their own minds forestalled the eagle's judgment, of giving the preference to the dove. 'Now, my good children,' said Mrs. Teachum, 'if you will pass through this life with real pleasure, imitate the dove; and remember, that innocence of mind, and integrity of heart, adorn the female character, and can alone produce your own happiness, and diffuse it to all around you.'

Our little company thanked their governess for her fable; and, just at that instant, they heard a chariot drive into the court, and Mrs. Teachum went out to see what visitor could be arrived so late in the evening; for it was near eight o'clock.

They all remained in the room where their governess left them; for they had been taught never to run out to the door, or to the windows, to look at any strangers that came, till they knew whether it was proper for them to see them or not

Mrs. Teachum soon returned with a letter open in her hand, and remained some little time silent; but cast on every one round such a tender and affectionate look, a tear almost starting from her eye, that the sympathising sorrow seemed to spread through the whole company, and they were all silent, and ready to cry, though they knew not for what reason. 'I am sorry, my little dears,' said Mrs. Teachum, 'to give your tender bosoms the uneasiness I fear the contents of this letter will do, as it will deprive you of that your hearts so justly hold most dear.' And, so saying, she delivered to Miss Jenny Peace, the following letter:—

'To Miss Jenny Peace.

'Monday night, June 24.

'My dear niece,—I arrived safe at my own house, with your cousin Harriet, last Saturday night, after a very tedious voyage by sea, and a fatiguing journey by land. I long to see my dear Jenny as soon as possible, and Harriet is quite impatient for that pleasure.

'I have ordered my chariot to be with you tomorrow night; and I desire you would set out on Wednesday morning, as early as your inclination shall prompt you to come to

'Your truly affectionate aunt,

'M. NEWMAN.

'I have writ a letter of thanks to your kind governess, for her care of you.'

It is impossible to describe the various sensations of Miss Jenny's mind, on the reading this letter. Her rising joy at the thoughts of seeing her kind aunt safely returned from a long and tedious voyage, was suppressed by a sorrow, which could not be resisted, on parting with such dear friends, and so good a governess; and the lustre which such a joy would have given to her eye, was damped by rising tears. Her heart for some time was too full for utterance. At last, turning to her governess, she said, 'And is the chariot really come, to carry me to my dear aunt?' Then, after a pause, the tears trickling down her cheeks, 'And must I so soon leave you, madam, and all my kind companions?' Mrs. Teachum, on seeing Miss Jenny's tender struggles of mind, and all her companions at once bursting into tears, stood up, and left the room, saying, 'She would come to them again after supper.' For this prudent woman well knew, that it was in vain to contend with the very first emotions of grief on such an occasion, but intended, at her return, to show them how much it was their duty and interest to conquer all sorts of extravagant sorrow.

They remained some time silent, as quite struck dumb with concern, till at last Miss Dolly Friendly, in broken accents, cried out, 'And must we lose you, my dear Miss Jenny, now we are just settled in that love and esteem for you, which your goodness so well deserves?'

Miss Jenny endeavoured to dry up her tears, and then said, 'Although I cannot but be pleased, my dear companions, at every mark of your affection for me; yet I beg that you would not give me the pain to see that I make so many dear friends unhappy. Let us submit cheerfully to this separation (which, believe me, is as deeply felt by me as any of you) because it is our duty so to do; and let me entreat you to be comforted, by reflecting, how much my good aunt's safe return must be conducive to my future welfare; nor can you be unhappy, while you continue with so good a governess, and persist in that readiness to obey her, which you have lately shown. She will direct who shall preside over your innocent amusements in my place. I will certainly write to you, and shall always take the greatest delight in hearing from each of you, both while you continue here, and when your duty and different connections shall call you elsewhere. We may some, and perhaps all, of us, happen often to meet again; and I hope a friendship, founded on so innocent and so good a foundation as ours is, will always subsist, as far as shall be consistent with our future situations in life.'

Miss Jenny's friends could not answer her but by sobs and tears; only little Polly Suckling, running to her, clung about her neck, and cried, 'Indeed, indeed, Miss Jenny, you must not go; I shall break my heart, if I lose you: sure we shan't, nor we can't, be half so happy, when you are gone, though our governess was ten times better to us than she is.'

Miss Jenny again entreated them to dry up their tears, and to be more contented with the present necessity; and begged, that they would not let their governess see them so overwhelmed in sorrow on her return; for she might take it unkindly, that they should be so afflicted at the loss of one person, while they still remained under her indulgent care and protection.

It was with the utmost difficulty, that Miss Jenny refrained from shedding tear for tear with her kind companions; but as it was her constant maxim to partake with her friends all her pleasure, and to confine her sorrows as much as possible within her own bosom, she chose rather to endeavour, by her own cheerfulness and innocent talk, to steal insensibly from the bosoms of her little companions half their sorrow; and they begin to appear tolerably easy.

After supper, Mrs. Teachum returned; and, seeing them all striving who should most conceal their grief, for fear of giving uneasiness to the rest, yet with a deep dejection fixed in every countenance, and little Polly still sobbing behind Miss Jenny's chair, she was so moved herself with the affecting scene, that the tears stole from her eyes; and the sympathising company once more eased their almost bursting hearts, by another general flow of melting sorrow.

'My dear children,' said Mrs. Teachum, 'I am not at all surprised at your being so much concerned to part with Miss Jenny. I love her myself with a motherly affection (as I do all of you, and shall ever continue to do so while you so well deserve it); and I could wish, for my own sake, never to part with her as long as I live; but I consider, that it is for her advantage, and I would have you all remember, in her absence, to let her example and friendship fill your hearts with joy, instead of grief. It is now pretty late in the evening, and as Miss Jenny is to set out very early in the morning, I must insist upon shortening your pain (for such is your present situation), and desire you would take your leave of this your engaging friend.'

They none of them attempted to speak another word, for their hearts were still too full for utterance; and Miss Jenny took every one by the hand as they went out of the room, saluted them with the tenderest affection, mingling tears with those which flowed from every streaming eye; and, wishing them all happiness and joy till their next meeting, they all, with heavy hearts, retired to rest.

Miss Jenny returned the warmest and most grateful acknowledgments to her good governess, for all her care of her; and said, 'I shall attribute every happy hour, madam, that I may hereafter be blessed with, to your wise and kind instruction, which I shall always remember with the highest veneration, and shall ever consider you as having been to me no less than a fond and indulgent mother.'

Mrs. Teachum kept Miss Jenny in the room with her no longer than to assure her how sincerely she should regret her absence, and confessed how much of the regularity and harmony of her school she owed to her good example, for sweetness of temper, and conformity to rules.

THE END OF THE NINTH DAY.
THE CONCLUSION OF THE HISTORY OF MRS. TEACHUM, &C.

Although Miss Jenny Peace did not return any more to school; yet she ever gratefully remembered the kindness of her governess, and frequently corresponded with all her companions. And as they continued their innocent amusements and meetings in the arbour, whenever the weather would permit, there was no day thought to be better employed than that in which they received a letter from their absent instructive friend, whose name was always mentioned with gratitude and honour.

Mrs. Teachum continued the same watchful care over any young persons who were entrusted to her management; and she never increased the number of her scholars, though often entreated so to do. All quarrels and contentions were banished her house; and if ever any such thing was likely to arise, the story of Miss Jenny Peace's reconciling all her little companions was told to them; so that Miss Jenny, though absent (by the bright example which she left behind her) to be the cement of union and harmony in this well-regulated society. And if any girl was found to harbour in her breast a rising passion, which it was difficult to conquer, the name and story of Miss Jenny Peace soon gained her attention, and left her without any other desire than to emulate Miss Jenny's virtues.

In short, Mrs. Teachum's school was always mentioned throughout the country, as an example of peace and harmony; and also by the daily improvement of all her girls, it plainly appeared how early young people might attain great knowledge, if their minds were free from foolish anxieties about trifles, and properly employed on their own improvement; for never did any young lady leave Mrs. Teachum, but that her parents and friends were greatly delighted with her behaviour, as she had made it her chief study to learn always to pay to her governors the most exact obedience, and to exert towards her companions all the good effects of a mind filled with benevolence and love.

CPSIA information can be obtained
at www.ICGtesting.com
Printed in the USA
LVOW01s1044190116
471181LV00029B/1357/P